The staircase /
YAF RIN

30776

Rinaldi, Ann.

W9-BSJ-316

The Staircase

Other Novels by Ann Rinaldi

The Coffin Quilt
The Feud between the Hatfields and the McCoys

Cast Two Shadows
The American Revolution in the South

An Acquaintance with Darkness

Hang a Thousand Trees with Ribbons
The Story of Phillis Wheatley

Keep Smiling Through

The Secret of Sarah Revere

Finishing Becca
A Story about Peggy Shippen and Benedict Arnold

The Fifth of March
A Story of the Boston Massacre

A Break with Charity
A Story about the Salem Witch Trials

A Ride into Morning
The Story of Tempe Wick

Ann Rinaldi

The Staircase

Gulliver Books • Harcourt, Inc.
San Diego   New York   London

Requests for permission to make copies of any part of the
work should be mailed to the following address:
Permissions Department, Harcourt, Inc.,
6277 Sea Harbor Drive, Orlando, Florida 32887-6777.

www.harcourt.com

Gulliver Books is a trademark of Harcourt, Inc.,
registered in the United States of America and/or other jurisdictions.

Library of Congress Cataloging-in-Publication Data
Rinaldi, Ann.
The staircase/by Ann Rinaldi.
p. cm.
Summary: In 1878, after her mother's death on the way west,
thirteen-year-old Lizzy Enders is left by her father at a convent school
in Sante Fe, where she must deal with being the only non-Catholic student
and where she plays a part in what some consider a miracle.
[1. Catholic schools—Fiction.   2. Schools—Fiction.
3. Fathers and daughters—Fiction.   4. Sante Fe (N.M.)—Fiction.]   I. Title.
PZ7.R459Sp 2000
[Fic]—dc21   00-8854
ISBN 0-15-202430-1

Text set in Simoncini Garamond
Designed by Lori McThomas Buley

First edition
A C E G H F D B

Printed in the United States of America

In memory of my mother
1902–1934

The Staircase

MY FATHER WAS digging the grave, with one arm. I watched his labors. We all did, especially Elinora, who stood beside me.

"He ought to hang your mother between tree branches, like the Indian skeleton we saw back a ways," she said. "So the wolves don't get her."

"My mama's not going to hang between any trees. So hush your mouth, Elinora."

"He could bring her on with us. My uncle would give her a proper burial."

"Santa Fe is days away yet." I wished we could bring Mama along, too, and not leave her in this godforsaken place. But I knew better than to say anything to Daddy right then. And I wasn't about to let Elinora know I agreed with her. Or hear any more about her stupid uncle, the Bishop.

My father was breathing heavily from his efforts. Every so often he'd stop, mop his face with his dirty handkerchief, and go on. Was he wiping away tears? I tried to see but couldn't.

I had no tears myself. We'd had a burial ceremony less than an hour ago. We'd sung Mama's favorite hymn. But the sound was weak against the rising wind, which carried it away in the vastness like a ball of tumbleweed. We'd be here forever, the way Daddy was proceeding. The indifferent reddish earth was slipping right back into the hole even as he dug.

"Mr. Enders, you must let me help." It was Mr. French. He stepped forward. He and his wife, Ida, and their twin boys were traveling with us in their own wagon, where the boys now slept. In a third wagon were the Wades. His wife, Nancy, was only sixteen, three years older than me. And she with a baby.

"Poco a poco," Daddy said. Little by little. He knew Spanish. He handed his shovel to Mr. French. "Damned ground is full of the dust of old bones," he said.

Mr. French dug and dug and dug. The ground seemed to resist his efforts, as if it did not want my mother. As if it knew her time had come too soon. The sound he made digging was a soft thud. It was useless here—all sound was, even our voices. There was nothing to measure them against.

We were insignificant in this endless country that seemed to go on forever. Only the distant mountains gave us an idea of our size. Now they were trimmed in the gold of aspens, the sky darkening behind them.

It was the starkness of the country that had bothered Mama so much. She'd told me that in her last days as she lay feverish on her bed in the wagon as we jogged along. "There is no end to it, Lizzy," she said. "It is eternity."

For her it was. I heard her whimpering at night when a coyote howled. Once, when we passed an old Indian wrapped and unmoving in a blanket while sitting in front of a pueblo, she clutched my hand. "He's waiting for me, Lizzy," she said.

She died the next day, of the putrid fever. She who came from Georgia, where the days make you feel as if you are being

bathed in milk. And then later, after all that Georgia business—
after the war that took Daddy's arm in the Battle of Buzzard
Roost Gap, after the milk turned sour for her—it was to Independence, Missouri. To the arms of her family that sheltered
her so. And nearly squeezed the life out of Daddy.

"Mr. Wade should help," Elinora whispered savagely.
"Rain is coming. And you know how fast night falls."

I knew she was wishing the whole thing over and done
with for herself. She wanted supper; she wanted to get into her
soft nightdress and get the best place in the wagon. She did not
wish to forgo her comforts. Each night as darkness came on,
she scuttled into our wagon, frightened of every shadow.

"Hush your mouth, or I'll put a scorpion in your gravy
tonight," I threatened.

She gasped. "You would, too, you...you—oh, if your
mother hadn't just died! And here at her holy grave site you
make threats!"

"There's nothing holy about any of this," I told her.

"For shame! Your mother's grave is holy!"

"It's nothing of the kind. No grave is."

"Oh, and you're such a heathen. Not even to grieve her!
You need to come to school with me, Lizzy Enders. You need
the Sisters of Loretto. I'm going to tell your father!"

"You do and I'll make you sorry you ever drew breath!"

All this went on in whispers, but Daddy must have heard
some of it. He gripped my shoulder, thinking I was taken with
grief. I did not yet know what grief was. That would come
later. "I'm all right, Daddy," I said. He let go.

I looked up at him, at the sharp outline of his face that had
once been handsome. And at the eyes, which Mama said had
once seen hell in the war and still recollected what it looked

like and that's why they were so sad. I looked at the empty shirtsleeve, pinned up.

I felt some of my old love for him rising in my breast. I had covered it over with anger when we left Independence, anger for taking me and Mama away. On different days coming west, I had tried to keep that anger, like a fire in the wind. Because it was safer than feeling anything else. Uncle William, one of grandfather's half-Indian sons, had once told me that.

"Keep your anger if you can keep nothing else, Lizzy," he had said. "People will respect you more for anger than for tears."

So, I was trying to keep it.

But most of the time all I felt was confusion. How could you love and hate somebody at the same time? I did not know what I felt about my father anymore. But I knew you shouldn't be halfway in your feelings. Uncle William had said so. And you couldn't be halfway in such country as this. The shapes and colors, the unforgiving earth, the sky, the rocks, the flowering cactus, the dust storms, the sudden appearance of knee-high lilacs in the middle of all the deadness, the howling wind at night, wouldn't let you be halfway about anything.

You had to feel something. One way or the other. It was demanded of you.

The land changes all the time, right in front of your eyes. It's the light that changes things. You learn not to trust the light. One minute you are seeing heights and depths that are ragged and harsh and jutting out in threatening lines, and the next, everything is bathed in pink and purple and gray, soft and innocent and pulling you in.

Mr. French was finished digging. Darkness was coming on fast, though over some mountain peaks in the west there was light, like midday. I moved closer as Mr. French helped Daddy pick up the buffalo robe with Mama in it and set it into the grave. In the distance I heard a coyote wail.

"Say good-bye to your mama, Lizzy," Daddy directed. He was standing over the buffalo robe. Elinora was reading something from her Bible. I wished she would shut up. I liked the howling of the coyote better. It was more fitting.

I stood respectfully for a minute, but it had nothing to do with Mama. I did not feel her presence inside that buffalo robe. She was gone already, away from this place. I wished I could be.

But I turned as I knew I must and went to help Mrs. French and Mrs. Wade with the supper.

2

❖

I COULDN'T EAT SUPPER that night. It didn't seem right, with Mama lying in her grave just a bit away from us. Nobody pushed me, though Mrs. French did say, "Lizzy, on the Trail you eat and partake of water when you can, dear. It has nothing to do with wanting to. It has to do with staying alive."

I wasn't so sure just then that I wanted to stay alive. Then I looked at Daddy bent over the fire, staring into it, not eating, either, and I thought, *I have to stay alive for him. Mama would want it. Can't let him go on his own. He himself forgets to eat sometimes.*

"Leave her be," Daddy said. And, for the moment, I felt my old love for him.

Left be, I just sat there and gazed out, past the fire in the pit, at Mama's grave and wondered what her family would think of her lying here in the shadow of the Sangre de Cristo Mountains, when she'd been so alive and lovely back in Independence, growing her roses in the garden, starting the women's literary guild, and baking all those cakes for the church fairs.

"Will you write Uncle William and tell him she's dead?" I asked Daddy. He said he would, soon's we got to Santa Fe.

I wondered what Uncle William would say. Mama was his favorite sibling. Yet he'd approved of our trip. But then, he was an adventurer. For the most part he ran Bent's New Fort on the Mountain Branch of the Santa Fe Trail. But the house in Independence had been his; Mama had run it for him. And when he came home it had been so exciting. He'd sometimes bring friends from Fort Bent. And gifts. He had brought my pony, Ben.

Mama was a Bent. Her family was of consequence in Independence. Her father had been a fur trapper, who'd become rich and had three Indian wives. I'd once met the last one, Grandma Adalina, a Blackfoot, at the time of Grandpa William's death.

I have Cheyenne and Blackfoot cousins that I don't even know. And I'm thirteen already.

I have some Blackfoot in me. Mama always said it was the part that didn't cry when other girls did. But by the time I came along I think it was probably washed clear out of my blood. By the time I came along the family had lost most of its wealth, though they still owned the largest mercantile business in Independence. Mama's brothers still traded in furs, sold blankets from New Mexico, drove New Mexican sheep to Missouri, and traded horses and mules.

After the war General William Tecumseh Sherman wanted to give Negro families forty acres of land each, on the coast and riverbanks from Charleston, South Carolina, to Jacksonville, Florida. So he issued General Order Number 15. I was just born. Mama and Daddy told me how he took our plantation, which he'd ruined, anyway, and gave it to the

Negroes. So Daddy and Mama went to Independence. Mama's family gave Daddy a job in their mercantile. We lived in their large house, with the porch that went all the way around. Uncle William was always off somewhere having adventures, so the house was mostly ours. But Daddy went about with his spirit cast down because he could no longer keep a roof over his family's heads.

One day a gunman came to the store and held Daddy up. Daddy had refused to use a gun since the war. The man got away with the robbery. Uncle William was disappointed that Daddy couldn't hold the robber off. And I was disappointed that the robber wasn't Jesse James. I would have been the envy of every girl in Independence if he had been. And somehow it was never the same in the house in Independence again.

Finally Daddy said there was nothing for it, we must go west. To seek gold in Colorado's hills. Mama wanted to stay in Independence. She didn't want to leave her brother's home, her church, her friends, her literary ladies. How she cried. How I cried.

I was crying because my Best Friend Ever Cassie was there. Cassie's mother was soon to have a baby, and Cassie and I had talked for hours of how we'd care for it. I always longed for a little sister. Now I missed the tree-lined streets of Independence, the stores, the steepled brick courthouse, the constant flow of emigrant wagons coming through—the way their drivers would shoot off guns to announce their arrival and everybody would go out to greet them. Sometimes we'd take a weary family into our home for the night.

When we left I knew I'd never see Cassie again. She ran after the wagon, crying. I hung over the tailgate, reaching for the paper she was holding out to me. I just managed to grab it. "Don't open until you are lonely," she yelled.

I watched her until she was a small speck in the dust, and then I opened it. It was her very best reward poster for Jesse James. The one issued by the Pinkerton men right after he robbed the Missouri-Pacific Railroad of over fifteen thousand dollars.

Tacked onto it was a small bit of paper. *I know you will cherish this. I'll take care of your cats, don't worry.*

I had to leave my cats behind with Cassie. I had three, and a whole passel of kittens. I begged to be allowed to take one kitten, but Daddy said no. Oh, how I would have loved just one kitten!

I was allowed to take Ben, my saddle pony, for he'd be useful on the Trail. I rode him beside the wagon. But then Elinora would get jealous and cry. I never saw such a girl for crying. So I had to sit in the wagon with her or let her ride Ben. Once she fell off and near killed herself, so Mama wouldn't let her ride anymore. After all, you couldn't deliver a girl with a broken head to an archbishop.

Bishop Jean Baptiste Lamy knew Mama's family. And though we weren't Catholic, he knew Mama was a good church lady and Daddy wanted to make a trip to trade on the Gila Trail, then head for Colorado. So the Bishop wrote and asked Daddy to make a stopover at Santa Fe and bring his grandniece to the girls school there. He was the bishop of the whole Southwest, Daddy said. And he would pay well for safe delivery of Elinora. So Daddy saw his way not to accept any money from Mama's brothers for our trip. With our caravan we had four mules, carrying cargo, books and paper, and supplies for the girls school—cutlery, dinnerware, woolens and calico, even canned goods.

The whole trip up to the time Mama died took fifty days. And we still had more to go. We could have taken the train to southeast Colorado, the farthest point the railroad went. But Bishop Lamy wrote that he wanted his grandniece to "witness the travel on the Santa Fe Trail," as he had so often done, before the railroads took over.

Elinora knew, all the while, that she was Miss Importance on this trip. Every whim of hers was satisfied. If she wanted to stop and pick wildflowers, we did so. Mama and I shared the same basin of water to wash as we crossed fifty miles of dry plain, but Elinora would have her own. At Fort Union Mama was already sick, but Elinora must be taken through the fort to see it.

Only one time did she not get her way. She had wanted to travel the Mountain Branch route to see Bent's New Fort and all the trappers, Indians, and military men there. Daddy said no. The Cimarron Cutoff was a hundred miles shorter. But I think the real reason was because Daddy just didn't want to see Uncle William.

I WAS FEEDING BEN and seeing to him for the night when I noticed Elinora talking with Daddy a bit away from the fire. She wanted something again. Probably to stop tomorrow at some stream and do a watercolor for her uncle. She had her drawing paper and watercolors with her. She fancied herself an artist. I know Daddy wanted to get on with the trip. It was already the beginning of October.

Oh, it would be so good getting shut of Elinora.

I stayed awhile with Ben. I had a bit of sugar for him. I put my face close to his, and he knew I was grieving. Horses know. *Animals know*, Mama always said.

"We're going on to Colorado," I told him. "We're going to find gold, and someday we'll come back here and find Mama and take her home for a proper burial."

By the time I got into the wagon, Elinora was already snuggled—in my traveling bed, the one Mama had made by sewing two comforters together. One side was lined with a warm Indian blanket and the other was covered with canvas so water would roll right off it.

"It's going to be cold tonight," Elinora said. "You wouldn't want me to come down with the fever, would you? Your daddy promised my uncle I'd be delivered safely."

"Keep the old thing," I said. "I'll use Mama's." My mother had made one for herself, too.

"See that fire outside? Your daddy's burning it because your mama died of the fever." She pulled up part of the wagon canvas so I could see the fire. It was sending sparks into the surrounding dark.

I settled down on the other side of the wagon, in some quilts, with a pillow. Oh, how I wished I had a kitten! I heard the murmur of voices outside as the others settled into the wagons. My daddy would take the first watch, then sleep under our wagon. A dog would do, I decided. Maybe on the way to Colorado Daddy would let me get a dog.

I ached for Mama, for the way she'd always kiss me good night. The pain was like what Daddy had told me his pain had been when he'd first lost his arm—and sometimes still was. An aching of the part of you that was not there anymore. How could that be, I'd wondered when he first told me. Now I knew.

"Do you want to talk about your mama?" Elinora's voice came across the dark.

"No, I want to be left alone."

"You can't go on to Colorado with your daddy, you know."

"And why not?"

"It isn't right, a girl our age going to Colorado. There's

nothing there but miners and Indians and saloons and bawdy houses. No real homes or real people."

"My daddy is real people."

"He's too addled to take care of you."

"He's not addled. Anyways, I don't need taking care of."

"You go there, you'll be doing laundry in a tub of cold water. Eating in a saloon. There's no churches, no proper families."

I snuggled into my quilts. "What do you care?"

"No need to be Miss Sassy-Boots. I'm only trying to help."

"I don't need your help, thank you. Now I need to sleep so I can get up early and help put stones on Mama's grave so when we leave the wolves don't get into it."

Elinora made a shuddering sound. "How you can talk so," she said. "You've lost all sense of propriety. My mama's been dead since I was ten, and you don't see me being boorish, do you?"

"I hope, shortly, not to see you at all, Elinora."

"I'm suffering this from you only because you just lost your mama. I'm offering it up."

"You do that."

"You're blasphemous, too. The Sisters will be shocked when they meet you."

"They won't meet me if I can help it."

"You do get over it, you know. Your mother dying. She's in heaven with God. You should be happy for her."

"I'd be happier if she was here, Elinora. God doesn't need her, and I do."

"Oh, sweet Mother of God."

I knew she was crossing herself. She'd come from a convent school in St. Louis. She was all the time saying her beads and showing me pictures of saints with fire around their heads and their eyes cast to heaven. I knew them just from her telling: Saint Theresa. Saint Agnes. And some man saint all pierced with arrows, like he'd been attacked by Comanches.

Worse yet, her last name was St. Clair. Her mama was the Bishop's niece, had gone to school in Santa Fe herself and taken it all so seriously she'd gone and married somebody with a saint's name.

"Of course, your mama's likely in a Methodist part of heaven, and that isn't as good as the Catholic part. But I'm sure she's very happy."

"If you don't hush up, Elinora, I'm going to take those beads of yours and wrap them around your neck!" I meant it. She didn't hush, though. It'd take more than that to make her.

"Did you know that years ago my uncle met Kit Carson?"

I did not answer.

"Did you know there are two witches who live in Santa Fe who dispense love potions?"

I turned over on my quilts, hating her.

"I already know how to make a love potion. You mix herbs, powders, cornmeal, and worms. They can be fried or mashed, it doesn't matter. Then you put some urine of the person you want to love you in it."

"How do you get that?" I demanded.

"What?"

"The urine of the person you want to love you. How do you get it?"

"Well, if you're going to split hairs, Lizzy Enders, when I go to visit the witches in Santa Fe, you can't come with me."

"I won't be there, so you can *live* with them as far as I'm concerned."

"Don't be so sure that it won't happen."

"What?"

"Never mind. Did you know that my-uncle-the-Bishop once fought off an attack by Comanches? It was just after the war. On his way home to Santa Fe after a trip to Rome, he picked up some Jesuit priests and some nuns in Ohio. Their wagon train was attacked by Comanches along the Arkansas River. Some men traveling with him were killed, but he was right out front fighting, shooting his six-guns, for six hours. And they finally beat the Comanches back."

Well, I thought, *then maybe he'll be a match for you.*

I heard her turning over in my traveling bed. I never thought I could hate anybody so much in my whole life as I hated Elinora St. Clair that night. My whole body shook with sobs of hatred for her. At least that was what I told myself my body was shaking from. But I buried my face in the pillow so she wouldn't hear me.

3

❖

NEXT MORNING I WOKE to the sound of hammering. Damn, I'd overslept. No, I mustn't let Elinora hear me say *damn*. I'd learned that word in Independence, from Uncle William. Mustn't let Daddy hear me say it, either. It would give him one more thing to dislike Uncle William for, and he disliked him enough already.

No matter, Elinora was still sleeping. I got up, dressed quietly, and crept out of the wagon.

It was cold. October-morning cold. Grave cold. The sun was only a red promise in the east. To the north the Sangre de Cristo Mountains looked like jagged edges of black tar paper torn off a shack. The kettle was on the fire. Mrs. Wade was bending over a frying pan. I smelled bacon. I was about starved.

Daddy was hammering a rude cross into the ground over Mama's grave. The sound carried, made bigger than it was, like everything else out here. All around us in the vastness were shapes. By the light of day they would likely be stunted cedar trees on a flat mesa. But now they could be witches or

15

crouching Indians. Whatever the mind made them. I shivered. The whole place brooded.

A pile of stones was nestled at my father's feet. I went over to help set them about Mama's grave. A nagging thought clouded my head. No, it was the filmy leftover bits of a dream. What had I dreamed? It came to me in pieces. Something about cutting off the ears of mules. Then I remembered. William Becknell had cut off the ears of his mules to drink their blood when crossing the fifty-mile dry plain. Elinora had told me that story. I shuddered, kneeling on the cold ground, setting the stones on top of Mama.

"Daddy?"

"How are you this morning, Lizzy?"

"I'm right fine, Daddy. How long to Santa Fe?"

"Three or four days now."

"Daddy, I had a dream last night. It sticks in my mind like glue."

"What is it, Lizzy?"

"About cutting off the mules' ears like Becknell did."

"Who told you that story?"

"Elinora."

"That girl does have a sense of drama."

"Daddy, you aren't going to leave me in Santa Fe and go off to Colorado alone, are you?"

He was using a rock as a hammer. He slammed it violently atop the cross. "Don't know what good this soil is for anything out here."

"Did you hear me, Daddy?"

"Yes, I heard you, Lizzy."

"Well, you ain't going to leave me, are you?"

"Don't say *ain't*. Or I'll have to leave you with those nuns.

You've had better schooling. Your mama would turn over in her grave right now if she heard you."

I finished with the last of the stones and stood up. "Then you aren't going to leave me?"

He threw the rock down, shook the top of the cross to test its firmness, dusted his one hand off on his pants, and turned in the direction of the fire. "Now, why would I do such, Lizzy?"

But it wasn't a real question. And it wasn't an answer, either. His voice had taken on that indifferent tone he used when he was lying. I stood there near Mama's grave, watching the others gather for breakfast. The Wades' twin boys were up, jumping around and demanding food. Mrs. French's baby whimpered, and she went off a piece to open her dress and nurse it.

I should help, I told myself. I went to the fire and picked up two tin plates and heaped them with bread and bacon and beans for the Wade boys. I took only some coffee and bread for myself. Somehow I couldn't eat now. Something sat where my stomach should be. And I recognized it for what it was.

Fear. And knowing. The same fear and knowing I'd had when Mama took sick. The kind that finds a home in your bones.

The milk was all gone, so I put extra sugar in my coffee, but I tasted nothing. Mama had wanted to bring a cow along, but Daddy had said no. Once or twice we'd been able to stop at farms and buy some milk.

Elinora came out of the wagon, blinked, rubbed her eyes, and took the coffee and plate of food handed to her by Mrs. Wade. "No milk," Elinora complained. "I hate coffee without milk."

"Likely we'll get some goat's milk the next spread we run into," Daddy told her. She was sitting next to him on a blanket. He set down his coffee to put his arm around her shoulder, and she smiled at him. I now felt fear and knowing and nausea, too.

We ate in silence, watching the day lighten. Then everybody but Elinora had chores.

I washed dishes. The Wade boys, though only seven, had fetched the water from a nearby creek and then had gone to get more to carry on the wagon. The Frenches put out the fire and spread water on it. And then from the corner of my eye I saw them spreading underbrush on top of the stones on Mama's grave. The Wades packed the mules. Daddy hitched up the oxen. I watched him. Never could I do anything but stop and wonder the way he did things with just one arm. Then he checked the wagons, making sure the water buckets, the feed box, everything was secure. Then came the "gee" and "haw" and "wo ho" to the animals, and we were off.

If I recollect anything about that day besides the tearing disbelief inside me that I would never see Mama again—that we were really leaving her there under the stones—it was that Daddy scarce spoke to me or looked at me. And every time I happened to engage his eyes, he'd look away.

THE NEXT DAY I carved my name on a rock. We stopped to "noon," as I was told the trail travelers called it. And the rock was there on a mound. Daddy was writing a letter, likely to Uncle William. I took a knife and walked off to the rock and carved my name. LIZZY. OCTOBER, 1878.

"Somebody will think you're buried under it," Elinora said.

So I said, "Let them."

We ran over two rattlesnakes with our wagons that afternoon, and later on in the day I saw some antelope. You could scarce make them out from the desert brush. "I wonder," I told Elinora, "if after you live out here awhile you start to blend into the background like they do."

She scoffed and said we were all made in God's image. "And He doesn't look like an antelope."

"How do you know?" I asked her. She had no reply.

That night, when we were at supper, an Indian walked into our camp. Elinora screamed, but I didn't. It seemed as if I just looked up and he was there, a dark figure against the red and purple streaks of sunset. At that time of night you can look up and expect to see anything, so I was not surprised.

He said he was an Arapaho. He spoke both Spanish and English and looked longingly at our stew pot and bread. My father offered him some food, and he sat right down and ate it, taking care first to take off his quiver of arrows. He wore a striped blanket and beads. He had long sleek hair tied in a piece of red felt. He said he was not looking for trouble, just food. So we let him eat. I felt curiously at peace with him sitting there outlined by the sunset, though Elinora took her food and went into the wagon.

He smiled at the French baby and then looked at me. Several times while I ate I felt his eyes upon me. Then when he finished, he put his bowl down, thanked the grown-ups, and came to put his hand on my head. "This one is wise," he said. "This one has an old spirit. She has been among us before."

I know I should have been frightened out of my wits, but I wasn't. There was a slight movement to my left, and I knew that Elinora was peeking out of the canvas of the wagon. The

Indian still had his hand on my head. "She will meet the spirits," he said. "And they will know her for her good heart."

Then he turned and walked off into the deepening darkness of the desert. And it was as if he had never been. Everyone went about their business. Nobody spoke of him. I felt as if I had been in a dream.

THE REST OF THE trip nothing much happened except that, the next day, we saw a mirage.

It was our first, and we all stopped to stare at it.

Then, in the hush, came Elinora's voice. "It's only a false pond. Some say it is attributed to the fact that the sky appears to be below the horizon. Others say it is the effect of gas that comes from the sub-scorched earth."

We continued on our way. Never would I be so glad as to get to Santa Fe and be shut of Elinora.

Just outside Sante Fe, Mrs. French presented me with a new dress and bonnet. I'd seen her sewing them. But then, she sewed all the time, sitting up there in their wagon, when she wasn't reaching over to keep one of the twins from falling beneath the wheels and killing himself.

"I don't know what to say," I told her. The dress was the softest calico, trimmed at the neck with real lace she'd brought from Independence.

She smiled. "You have to look nice for the nuns," she said.

I gripped the dress in my hands, which had gone sweaty. And I knew. I looked into her plain face. The blue eyes, pale as some ancient fire, burned into me, unblinking, telling me. My voice failed, but I managed to get out a proper thank-you. Then I took the dress into our wagon and stuffed it under my quilts. Elinora still had my travel bed.

We arrived at Santa Fe in that mystical hour before dark. The aspen trees, turned gold already, were weighted with the added gold of the sunset. We passed under a great wooden arch. I heard a church bell in the distance, so faint I thought it was in my dreams. It sounded like tinkling broken glass. How long I'd waited to get to Santa Fe! How Mama and I had planned what we'd do here in the two days Daddy had promised us we would stay! I knew I must look at this place. At least for Mama.

I was disappointed. The houses were all small and squat, the color of red sand. Mongrel dogs wandered the streets. Goats and burros napped on the wooden walkways. Everywhere were Indians in blankets, Mexicans in blankets, and women in blankets. But the children, the children, it seemed, ran about in next to nothing.

"There's the Governor's Palace!" Elinora came from the inside of the wagon to push herself between me and Daddy on the seat. "Look!"

"It doesn't look like much of a palace to me," I said.

"There's the oldest church in America! San Miguel!"

Now that looked the part. The walls were cracked and held up by beams.

"Children are not allowed in there," Elinora whispered. "It may fall down. But the priests hold mass there. God won't let it fall on them."

"But he'd let it fall on children?" I asked. "Is that what they believe?"

"Hush, Lizzy," Daddy said. "It's tradition. And she is educating us. Go on, Elinora."

"Thank you, Mr. Enders. There's the central plaza!"

Elinora acted as if she'd been here before. I felt as if I was already trapped here forever. I looked but couldn't see. Saw but couldn't make any sense of it. The church bell was louder now. "That's 'Ave Maria'!" Elinora said, and crossed herself.

The bell was so loud I covered my ears. But the sound got through, anyway, echoing in my head, my blood, my bones, insisting and insisting on something. What?

Our caravan had stopped in front of a church. "Oh!" Elinora scrambled down, nearly killing herself. And then, out of the grillwork door of a building next-door, through which I could see a courtyard and a garden, came some black-dressed figures.

"We thought you'd never arrive! Thank the Lord! Elinora? Is this Elinora St. Clair?"

Elinora curtsied. "Yes, Sister. And you must be Mother Magdalena."

They embraced. I stumbled down from the wagon, my bones cramped, my eyes unaccustomed to all those red houses, to the sight of the ridges of the foothills in the distance fired up by the sunset and shadowed all at the same time, to the sunset, red and orange now.

"Isn't it lovely?" the woman called Mother Magdalena said to me. "The conquistadores named those mountains that catch the light of the sunset Blood of Christ."

They would, I thought. But I nodded politely, numbly. Then there were greetings all around, with nuns and girls coming out of the grilled doorway and helping with our things. Mexicans appeared, too, with their everlasting blankets, to unburden and take away the mules, to unload the wagons, to unhitch the oxen. The nuns and girls exclaimed over the Wade boys and the Frenches' baby. They took the sleeping baby inside and led Mrs. French and Mrs. Wade, saying something about tea. Then the one they called Mother looked around. "But where is your wife, Mr. Enders?"

The story was told, quietly, by Daddy. The Mother crossed herself, then hugged me and called me "dear child." Her black dress smelled musty yet homey at the same time. I allowed myself to be led inside. Tea sounded wonderful. I would even call the mountains Blood of Christ for a cup of tea with real milk, by now.

Rooms were all ready for us, the Mother said. The whole party would stay the night.

WE WERE TAKEN THROUGH cool rooms with tiled floors, and walls that were plastered with something called *jaspe*. It was very, very white, and against the bottom half of the walls was pasted a calico covering. "So the whitewash doesn't brush off on our dresses," a nun explained. There were settees on which were thrown Navajo blankets. There were deep, deep windowsills, and on every sill was a pot of red geraniums. Candles flickered all over. And whichever way we looked there were plaster saints praying, bleeding, dying, but always with smiles on their faces and their eyes cast to heaven. Some of them were almost life-size.

They gave me a room upstairs with Elinora. It had mosquito netting on the beds, rag rugs on the floor, and, of course, the usual plaster saints and geraniums. Our portmanteaus were on the floor.

On each of our beds was a dark purple dress, shapeless and long. "Oh, the school uniform!" Elinora held hers up, beaming.

A Mexican woman brought in a bowl and a pitcher of water and gestured to them. "Oh, yes, I must wash!" And without asking me where I'd wash, Elinora pulled off her dress and stood in her pantalets and chemise and commenced to wash herself.

I got down on the floor, opened my portmanteau, and took out the dress Mrs. French had made for me.

"You're not wearing that!" Elinora objected.

"Well, I'm not wearing that stupid purple thing, since I'm not staying."

"It's the school uniform. They wanted to give you a fresh dress. It's an honor to wear it."

"That's why I'm not."

Just then the Mexican woman came in again with another bowl and pitcher of water. I could have kissed her. I wasn't about to wash in Elinora's leavings. Quickly I pulled off my traveling clothes and washed myself, too. The soap was perfumed. And there was some kind of powder as well.

From belowstairs came the tinkling of a bell. "Supper," Elinora said.

I put on the dress from Mrs. French, struggled with the buttons, then followed Elinora downstairs. From another part of the house there came the chatter of young girls. I looked out the window on the landing and saw four or five of them crossing the courtyard. I paused. In the middle of the courtyard was a garden with a little pond. In it were floating lotus flowers. In the garden were many fruit trees.

"My uncle brought them from St. Louis years ago when they were but little switches," she said. "There are trees all over Santa Fe from their cuttings. Isn't the garden beautiful?"

I could not deny it. "What are those?" I pointed to a line of trees against the south wall.

"Tamarisk. They are very old. In the spring their blossoms are lavender pink."

"How do you know so much? Have you been here before?"

"No. My mother went to school here. She told me everything."

Chickens scratched in the garden and dogs slept in the shade. I saw two cats washing their faces serenely. One gray and one black and white. And I thought of mine at home. "Oh, I'd love to pet them," I said. There were benches all around. It seemed quiet and peaceful.

"You can pet them tomorrow. Let's go."

ELINORA WAS POUTING. The Bishop did not come to supper.

"He's away," Mother Magdalena said. "He is visiting far-flung parishioners."

"You see?" Elinora nudged me. "I told you he was important."

To my relief none of the other nuns were at the table. Just our caravan party and Mother Magdalena. A Mexican woman served. At least eight candles in very large tin saucers glowed on the long, polished table and made flickering light over the ceiling beams. The dishes were pewter, the bread homemade, the stew mutton. Wine was served to the men. Old Persian rugs were on the floor.

By the time Mother Magdalena said grace and a whispered prayer for my mother, it seemed that I'd been inside that room forever. That I'd been there before, gone away, and left part of myself there, and now had come back to retrieve it.

It was the mutton stew, I told myself. Or the homemade

bread or the cherry wine Daddy allowed me to sip. Maybe it was the sweet-smelling smoke from that strange log burning in the hearth at the end of the room. Its crackling sound mixed with the melodious voice of Mother Magdalena, the faraway sound in a house of someone practicing the violin, the tinkling of glass and silverware, all lulled me into a near trance.

She was telling us about the new chapel that had just been finished. "It took five years and cost the Bishop dearly. And now we discover there was no staircase built to the choir loft. Can you imagine?"

"Oh!" Elinora's fork clanked on her dish. "Where will I sing, then?"

Mother Magdalena smiled. "We've heard about your lovely voice, child. I'm afraid that for now, until we figure out what to do about a staircase to get to the choir loft, the whole choir must be in the back of the church."

"Oh, but my uncle wrote about the chapel being built! I so looked forward to singing in the choir loft. How could they leave the staircase out?"

"Nobody knows," Mother Magdalena said sadly. "It seems that if you don't stand right over these workmen today, you don't get what you bargained for. We are praying on the matter. As a matter of fact, we have started a novena to Saint Joseph."

"I'd like to see what he can do about it," Elinora grumbled, so low that only I could hear.

By that time both Wade boys had to be carried to settees at the end of the room, before the meal was finished. The French baby was set in a nearby cradle. I wondered why they were not taken upstairs. Darkness came upon the land outside, but the candles sparkled brighter than ever on the table, dripping tallow into the tin saucers. There was a special dessert, some kind of cooked fruit with something sweet glazed all over it. And cookies. I was allowed some coffee. There was foamy milk and shaved chocolate on top of it.

I thought of the black bittersweet coffee on the Trail, the times I had to share my bowl of water for washing with Mama. For a moment I looked to the end of the table at Mother Magdalena and could have sworn that it was Mama's face inside that starched wimple, smiling at me.

"Mama?" I heard myself say it. I know I saw her through the tears in my eyes. The tears that blurred out the faces of the Wades and the Frenches and my daddy.

Soft but firm hands were lifting me then, out of my chair. I was being carried across the room. From outside the windows I heard footsteps, laughter, scurrying feet; then I heard Mother Magdalena's voice behind. "Oh, you girls, if you hear any screams from the street this night, don't be frightened. At night Santa Fe is a different world."

I was mindful of being carried up the stairs in someone's strong arms. I smelled the tobacco my father used. *Why,* I thought, *Daddy's grown another arm.* I knew this place was magic. I sensed we were in the room I was to share this one night with Elinora. Then I was on the bed and someone was removing my shoes and unbuttoning my dress and slipping it off. I was set between sheets that smelled clean, smelled of fragrant cedar, but were rough to the touch. The last thing I heard was Elinora's voice.

"Thank you, I'll put out the candles."

Sleep pulled me into its canyon, which was dark and full of

shadows. There was a light at the far end, and outside I could see cactus with bulbs of yellow growth, yellow butterflies, and olive-yellow birds. There was such a yearning in my heart to reach them that I thought I would die. But I did not have the strength. *Tomorrow,* I thought, *I'll reach them tomorrow.*

4

❖

THERE WAS A SCREAM, long and fashioned out of agony. It pulled me from my sleep. I opened my eyes. The wagon was flooded with moonlight. Was it a coyote? Who was on guard outside the wagon? I hoped it wasn't Daddy. I heard voices.

I sat up. Everything was in the wrong place. Who had moved me to this part of the wagon? I looked around, saw a large chifforobe, ancient and looming. Saw a window. And then I remembered.

"Elinora?" I whispered.

From her bed came the sound of snoring. She often snored at night. I pushed my covers back and got out of bed. The room was chilled with the breath of my own fear. I walked to the window and looked out.

Below me was the Santa Fe street, rich in moonlight and spilled shadows. People were moving around down there. Their voices carried on the night air, even through the windowpanes.

They were moving around the wagons of our caravan. They were hitching up the oxen and putting the packs on the mules.

Our caravan was leaving!

For a moment I could not think. Was it morning already? Who had screamed? I remembered then what Mother Magdalena had said about Santa Fe being different at night and that we shouldn't be afraid if we heard screams from the street.

Had my people made arrangements to leave before first light? That was it! They'd made arrangements after I fell asleep and had forgotten to tell me. Or would soon send the Mexican woman to wake me. I must dress!

I stood in the middle of the room in confusion and terror. Where were my traveling clothes? My hands fumbled as I lit a candle. I'd wake Elinora, but too bad. The candle gave scant light, but I could find my way around better. Where had I put my traveling dress yesterday? On that chair by the chifforobe. I turned to get it.

It was not there. Only the purple school uniform lay neatly over the back of the chair with my petticoats and shoes nearby. Very well, then I'd wear the calico Mrs. French had made for me. I whirled around, holding the candle. It, too, was nowhere in sight.

I ran again to the window. I could make out each of our party by the way they walked and held themselves. Mrs. French was holding the baby. The two Wade boys were being lifted into the family's wagon. And my daddy, tall, lanky, with one arm and that odd way he had of walking, as if to diminish his size, like an apology because he was always taller than everybody.

I ran then to the chifforobe and pulled at the door. My traveling dress would be inside. I must dress quickly. But the door would not open. I pulled and pulled at it, broke a nail, then banged. "Open, damn you!"

Elinora sat up in bed. "What is it? What's wrong?"

"They're leaving! Our caravan is leaving. Why didn't you tell me?"

"I didn't know."

"Liar! Stinking, prayer-lips liar!"

She got out of bed. "Lizzy, stop it."

"Get away from me; I've got to get dressed." I sat down and began to pull on my shoes, to button them up. I was still in my pantalets and chemise. Then I grabbed the purple school uniform from the chair and flung it over my head, grabbed my portmanteau and dragged it from the room.

"Lizzy, don't go like that. It's dark. You'll kill yourself."

"Not likely with all these damn candles in front of these saints in the walls," I sputtered as I went down the stairs. In the large foyer, I set down my portmanteau and ran to the immense grillwork door. I pulled on the handle.

It would not open. It was locked. Damn!

"Lizzy!" Elinora's frantic whisper followed me. "Hush, you'll wake everyone."

"I'll wake the dead if I have to." I struggled with the door, but it wouldn't budge. "Where do they keep the key?"

"I don't know."

"Stop lying to me, why don't you! I know you want me to stay here. Likely you fixed it with my father! Well, I'm not staying. Do you understand? Daddy!" I pounded on the door and pounded. "Daddy, I'm coming. I'm coming! Wait for me!"

If somebody would only stop that screaming, I thought, *he could hear me. Who is that screaming out in the street, anyway?*

And then, in the next instant, I knew. Great black wings came down as if from heaven and enveloped me. I smelled the mustiness of a nun's habit.

"Hush, you'll wake the whole house."

It had been me screaming. My throat was hoarse. I looked up into the stern face of Mother Magdalena.

"I want my father," I said. "Go outside and tell him I'm coming along directly. Please."

Her great blackbird arms held me close. She was all bosom and softness, and for a moment I thought, *Nobody has held me like this since Mama died.* And I near let her black wings carry me off. Then I caught myself and struggled. "No, no, you don't understand; they forgot to wake me. It's dark out there. My daddy thinks I'm in the wagon already. Go and tell him I'm not. Go and tell him he's forgotten me."

"He hasn't forgotten you, Lizzy. He has decided to leave you with us. He couldn't tell you himself. He thought this was the best way."

I knew it, of course. The knowing had been like a knife cutting into me for days now. I'd been bleeding for days from the knowing, and had refused to acknowledge it.

"Please, please, please," I sobbed. "Tell my daddy I have to go with him to Colorado. He needs me. Tell him I can't stay here."

"He needs you here, Lizzy," Mother Magdalena said. "He needs what's best for you."

"Please, just let me out to say good-bye then. Why didn't he even say good-bye?"

"I told you. He couldn't."

I sobbed. I begged. I, who had Cheyenne and Blackfoot in me, which was the part that never cried. I, who never begged for anything. Then all of a sudden I stopped. From outside came the shouts of "gee" and "haw" and "wo ho."

They were leaving.

"Noooo!" My scream was now as piercing as the one in the street before. Mother Magdalena held me while I struggled. Finally I managed to break free, and when I did, I went at Elinora. "I hate you!" I screamed. "You pious little buffalo chip!" I smacked her right in the face.

Such howling you never did hear, then. It was better than the poor soul who'd woken me from the street.

"No, no, that is no way to solve our problems," Mother Magdalena said severely. "Violence is no solution to anything."

"It is for me."

Elinora was sobbing, like she'd been scalped by a Comanche. And the sound of it did my soul good. Nuns came running from all directions then, it seemed, and helped Elinora off to bed. But before she went she turned at the foot of the stairway and aimed her words at me like arrows. "Why? Why would you want to go with a father who sneaks off without even saying good-bye? That's what I want to know!"

I slumped to the floor. Moonlight flooded in all around me. From outside came the last of the sounds of the caravan, the jingling of harnesses and creaking of wagon wheels. Then it was silent. Except for another piercing scream. But I knew from the way my throat felt now that the scream was not from the street outside but from me.

I WANTED TO STAY in bed the next morning, but they wouldn't allow it. As soon as I opened my eyes I saw a nun bending over me with a candle, saying something about holy mass. I pulled the covers over my head. I hurt; my throat hurt from screaming, my head hurt from not enough sleep, and my heart ached from betrayal. To think that everyone in the caravan knew my father was going to leave me! How long had they known? And Elinora! Of course, she'd known. Likely she'd talked him into it!

I hated her so much, it throbbed in my blood. Had everyone in the convent known, too? Oh, the hurtfulness of it! I was so shamed!

They made me get up. Elinora was dressed already, prattling on about singing at mass. Were they crazy? It was still dark. I stumbled, caught myself, and sat down again on the bed. The room was freezing with the night's chill, the fire in the grate low. Somehow I dressed and combed my hair and used the chamber pot. They were waiting for me in the hall.

By candlelight the statues in the wall crevices seemed to leer at me. *This is a convent,* they seemed to say. *You are here, whether you like it or not. A convent.*

I felt nauseous. My head throbbed. Weren't they even going to have breakfast? I longed for a cup of tea. I allowed Elinora to lead me to their new chapel for mass. I did not know about mass. I'd never been to one. The church was small, and I don't know why they called it a cathedral. But with these Catholics, you never knew anything.

The girls who didn't board at the school were coming in from outside. Some with parents. There seemed to be an army of them, all in purple uniforms with blankets around them. They all looked the same.

The incense gave me a headache. The mumblings of the priest sounded like Indian chanting. All they needed were some drums. On the altar there were boys in dresses, kneeling, ringing bells, and once when one turned around, I caught him winking at me. Oh, the brass of him! I turned away as if to escape, but I was in between two nuns. The mustiness of their habits filled my nostrils. They made responses to the priest in Latin.

They pulled me up and down, to stand, to kneel, to sit, to stand again. Couldn't they make up their minds? All this yanking of me was making my nausea worse. *Serve them right if I throw up on them,* I thought.

I looked for Elinora. I'd rather throw up on her. But as soon as we'd come in, she had disappeared. Now I knew why. From behind me came singing, soft at first. It was in Latin and the sound was like that which came from behind stone walls, down the centuries. Then I heard Elinora's voice, clear, piercing, reaching impossible notes. I turned. She was standing out in front of the others, her mouth making round exaggerated movements. Well, so she could sing. She was still ugly. Her nose was too big and her spectacles made it look bigger.

Who cared if she could sing, anyway?

My head hurt, and I wanted to throw up and go back to bed and run out and grab Ben and follow Daddy, all at the same time.

Ben!

Where was Ben? The thought of him left me stunned, as though I'd run into a brick wall. Last night I'd been too dazed, and this morning too sick, to ask about him.

Was he here? With me? Or had my father taken him? I squeezed my eyes shut and tried to remember what I'd seen out the window in the middle of the night. Had Ben been tethered to the back of our wagon? I couldn't remember!

The nun jerked me to my feet. I stood as if in a trance, the candles and their reflections in the large gold cross on the altar blinding my eyes. *I must get out of here. I must find Ben.* If he wasn't here, I would die!

What kind of a person was I that I hadn't even given a thought to Ben until now? Suppose he needed me?

I started to move, but I was blocked in by nuns. "I'm going to be sick," I said.

The nun on my right took me out into the aisle then, stood with me next to her and knelt on one knee. They were always kneeling on one knee. *Genuflecting,* they called it. Then she turned and brought me out the side door and into the vestibule, where she turned me over to a servant. "Ramona, show her the privy."

The woman led me outside. Light was just streaking the east, and I could scarce see the outline of the outbuildings, like a child's charcoal drawing. "Where's the barn?" I asked.

She shrugged.

"I need to find my horse. Horse," I said again. And I neighed.

"Ah." She nodded. *"Caballo."*

"Yes. *Caballo."*

She pointed to the largest building, patted me, and said, *"Bonita, muchachita."* And I ran.

Servants were cleaning out the stalls, feeding the horses. There were several, and I ran through the center of the barn, dodging piles of manure and hay.

"Ben, Ben!" I called.

Oh, if he wasn't here I would die! I wouldn't stay another minute! But he was. I heard him neigh before I saw him. He was in the last stall, and I flung my arms around his neck and hung on for dear life. "Oh, Ben, Ben, I am so happy to see you! Ben, I'm sorry I didn't see you to bed last night. I didn't even think of you until just before! Oh, Ben, I don't deserve you. But if you weren't here I would just wither away."

I hugged him. I drank in the familiar scent of him, the smell of horse and all it meant to me. Rides at home in the fields outside the town limits of Independence. Rides with Uncle William when he was home. Rides with Daddy. And all the time I spent with Ben on the Trail. All the special treats Mama had given him. How she taught me to weave ribbons into his mane.

I wept, holding him. I wept for my past, which was all gone, irretrievable. And Ben understood. He nuzzled me, comforted me. *I'll still be with you.* I know that's what he was saying. *Maybe everybody else abandoned you, but I am here.*

"I'll feed you," I said. And I found some oats and held the bag while he nibbled away. Then I gave him some water. All the time, a plan was forming in my mind. While he was drinking I looked around and saw his blanket, saddle, and bridle. When he was finished I dressed him for a ride.

He got anxious with just the touch of the blanket on his flanks, knowing we were going to be off. In no time at all we were ready, and I led him out of the barn as if it was the most natural thing in the world, smiling at the Mexican servants.

Outside, there was still a morning star in the sky when I mounted him. I knew where the gate was to the street and saw that it was open. A delivery wagon was just leaving. I could still hear singing from the cathedral as I walked him through the garden, past the fountain, and down the path to the gate. Then a figure came out of the shadows, and I prepared to make a run for it. But it was Ramona.

"Is it right to the Santa Fe Trail?" I asked.

"*El camino,*" she said. And she pointed left.

Funny, I thought it was right. Well, I was confused last night. She was holding something out to me. "*Pan de maiz.*"

I knew what that meant—corn bread—because I smelled it. Still warm from the oven. And what else? She held out a small canteen. Coffee! Oh, the fragrance. I slipped off Ben and thanked her, hugged her. "Ramona, you're my friend," I said.

She nodded. Then she became agitated. "*Una madre,*" she said.

Madre? I knew that meant "mother." Was she saying she was sorry about my mother? No, she was pointing left, up to the hill at the end of town. "*Una madre,*" she said again. Then she clasped her hands together and cast her eyes to heaven as if begging. "*Una madre.*" She was entreating me to do something. Pointing me in the direction. Someone she knew was in danger. I nodded, mounted Ben, and patted her arm.

It wasn't enough. She stood in front of Ben, took his bridle gently, and led us through the gate, then pointed again up the street. I looked past row upon row of low adobe houses, with candles just now flickering in the windows, up to the mountains at the end of the street to what looked like a crumbling barricade. She wanted me to go there and fetch someone.

I nodded, clucked to Ben, and rode off.

5

❖

AS BEN AND I climbed the hill at the end of town, the wind picked up and worked against us. The higher we got, the stronger the wind became. I ducked my head. There were mists up here, too, close to the ground. And all around were crumbling walls of what looked like an old army post. There were even one or two abandoned and rusty cannons.

I thought of Fort Bent and Uncle William. Elinora had not spoken of a fort here. Of course, she wouldn't. She only spoke of churches and religion.

What was I supposed to be seeking? Had I understood Ramona? Was there someone up here who was lost? Or injured? Was it a place people came to pray? Or a place where I might someday bury my mother? Perhaps the nuns had told her my mother had died on the Trail.

As I went through an old tumbledown wooden archway, I made out the weatherworn painted sign, FORT MARCY.

Ben and I climbed higher and higher. All around now were ruins of an old two-story building, and fortifications in which were holes, the kind you could shoot through. It was colder up here, and the ground was uneven. Ben was stepping delicately over and around things. I looked down.

We were in what appeared to be a cemetery. There were some broken headstones, with the writing not even readable anymore. And loose rocks. Ben kicked one aside.

Rocks? I looked down in horror. They were not rocks. They were bones. Old bones that were coming up from the earth because rain and wind had worn the earth away.

Carefully I guided Ben out of the cemetery, then turned and looked down at the town. I could see all, like God could see all. The town was coming to life. People were moving about around the houses, and on the streets. But the plaza was still deserted. I had a grand view. And something about being so far above my troubles gave me a sense of peace. From below I heard the church bell ringing. The girls would be leaving mass now. I wondered if anybody would miss me.

I don't know what I had in mind when I saddled Ben. To get away. To ride on the Santa Fe Trail and find Daddy. But in my heart, I knew I could not do that. He had taken the Trail south this time. And I did not know the Trail south. I would become lost in the desert. I don't know in what direction I would have gone if Ramona hadn't entreated me to come this way.

"*Una madre,*" she'd said. Elinora had been studying Spanish to please the nuns, and I'd heard her say the Hail Mary in Spanish enough to know that *madre* meant "mother."

I remembered then what she'd given me, and reached for the sack. I opened the container of coffee. It was still hot. And there on the hill, in the ruins of the earthworks of Fort Marcy, I had my breakfast on Ben's back. Coffee and corn bread. Oh, it tasted so good! I sat munching and drinking, letting Ben have his head so he could seek out some dried grass and dandelions. There was still some mist farther up the hill, but for the most part the sun had broken through now. The day would become pleasant once the mist burned off. I heard some bird-calls, saw what I thought was an eagle.

The hot coffee and corn bread, the sense of being on my own, of being able to survey the town from up on high, gave me comfort. I did not know what I was going to do about being left at the convent. Maybe I would write to Uncle William and tell him to come and fetch me home.

Yes, that was it. I would write to Uncle William. Surely he would not leave me here.

I felt better and gulped the rest of my coffee. And then I heard the crying.

So low that at first I thought it was the wind. Or part of the spell of the weedy desolation and crumbled crosses around me. And then I heard it again.

"Ben, did you hear that? Somebody is here." I turned him in the direction of the crying. It was uphill, where the mist still clung. We made our way through, carefully, lest Ben step in a hole or trip on some bones.

Ben stopped, neighed, lowered his head, then raised it. "What is it?" I asked.

Then I saw a woman on the ground in front of me. She was wrapped in a Navajo blanket, kneeling in front of a headstone that was listing to one side.

"Oh, Robert, Robert," she was crying, "I must go now, son. I am long gone, and the nuns will be looking for me. What do you know about that? I fell asleep here. But it's all right. At least you weren't alone this night. Still, I must go."

At the side of the grave was a small cavelike structure made of stones. Inside was a lantern. The woman saw me, reached for the lantern, and held it in front of her. "Oh!" She gave a small scream. "Oh, who are you? Go away, please!"

"It's all right, ma'am," I said. "We're not going to hurt you."

"Did they send you? They did, didn't they, the nuns? To fetch me. Well, I won't go back. They'll lock me in my room for coming here alone. But what could I do? None of the girls would come with me. And I had to see Robert."

She was crying, weeping, gesturing—threatening and angry at the same time. I scrambled down off Ben to kneel on the ground beside her. She backed away, afraid. "No, no, don't touch me. I won't be touched by a Catholic. They put a spell on you. I won't be under their spell."

"All right, I won't touch you. See?" I held my hands away from her. "And anyway, I'm not Catholic."

"You're not?" She was disbelieving. "Everybody around here is. How can you not be?" She dropped her voice to a whisper. "They're all over the place, the Catholics. The whole town is crawling with them. I have to be so careful."

There was a light that was not quite right in her eyes. She was demented, poor thing. "I'm Methodist," I said.

"You aren't."

"Yes, when I bother to be anything. I'm not very good at it, though, I'm afraid. I haven't much use for religion right now. But I was raised Methodist. My mama was a church lady in Independence. That's where I come from. But she died on the Trail, coming here. And my daddy isn't anything since the war."

"The war?" She blew out the candle in the lantern and set it down on the ground. "My Robert was always afraid of the dark as a child. So I leave the lantern for him at night." She had come alert at the mention of the war. The look in her eyes became sharp. "Your daddy was in the war?"

"Yes. He lost an arm."

"I lost Robert. Here, this is his gravestone."

"Your husband?"

"No, my son. My only dear son. I come up here every day to leave flowers. And leave the lantern for the night. Sometimes I sneak food out of the kitchen. I came last night and fell asleep and never woke until this morning. First time I've ever done that." She smiled. "Robert didn't mind, though."

Her smile was so warm it made her whole face seem like a room full of candles that I had suddenly walked into. Her eyes twinkled. She was old, yes. She had wrinkles, but it was the kind of old I knew my own mama would have grown into if she'd had the chance. The kind of old that says, "Come now, there's nothing to be afraid of. Don't be frightened."

She was a fine-looking woman, too, or once had been. Her jaw had a round firmness, her teeth were still all in her head, and her nose had what my mama would have called an "aristocratic line."

I should get her home, back to the convent. She didn't belong here on the cold ground. She could be getting a chill at this very moment. "What is your name?" I asked.

"The nuns call me Mrs. Lacey. But you can call me Violette."

She was "*una madre*," the one Ramona had told me about. And she was missing from the convent.

"I'm Lizzy," I said. "Come along; let's go back to the convent together."

"No, no." She waved me off. "I'd just as lief stay here with Robert as go back to those nuns. Lock me in my room, they will, for running off alone. I'm not going back there, I tell you. I'd rather stay here."

"But you can't live here," I protested.

"And why not?"

"Because. You'll take sick. It gets cold. Because"—and I had a thought then—"because Robert wouldn't want you to. He'd want you to be where you're warm and safe."

"But if I go back they won't let me come and see him again," she whined like a child. "Mother Magdalena will make me wear the asafetida bag around my neck. It stinks."

"I've run off without permission, too," I told her. "But if they let me, I'll come with you to visit Robert."

Her eyes, which were baby blue, widened. "You? Who are you? I don't know you, do I?"

"You do now. I'm Lizzy Enders. And I've run off without permission. This very morning. I even left mass to do it. I'll probably be punished, too."

"You live at the convent?" She peered into my face. "I don't recollect you. You must be a new girl."

"Yes." I sighed, resigned to it. "I'm new."

"When did you come?"

"Last night."

"And you're Methodist?"

"Yes, when I'm anything."

She nodded, mulling it over. Then she spoke. "Will you speak for me if I go back with you? Will you tell Mother Magdalena you'll come here with me every day?"

"I'll speak for you," I said. "Come; we'll go back together."

WE MADE OUR WAY down the hill carefully. I walked Ben, since it wouldn't be seemly to ride, and I had to hold her arm firmly. "How did you ever get up this hill yourself?" I asked.

"Oh, when I come to visit my Robert it isn't difficult. Going down can be worse."

"Don't you mind all these bones on the ground?"

"Not if they don't mind me!" She laughed. "The dead can't hurt you as much as the living."

"How long have you been at the convent?"

She stopped and stared at me. "I don't recollect. Forever, it seems. I came here with my husband when they made this place." She gestured to the ruined fort around us. "Let me see, that was many years ago. My first husband died during the war. I didn't want Robert to fight, but he ran away and became a drummer boy. He was only sixteen when he died. They shipped his body to me here. I mourned him so. He was my only child, you know. Then, after my second husband died, I became ill. Sometimes—" She stopped and squeezed my arm. "Sometimes they say I'm not right in the head. But during those times it seems I'm happiest. Tell me, with the world the way it is today, do you like being right in the head?"

I giggled. "Not always."

"Well, you see? When you're old you can go out of your head and get away with it. Not when you're young, though. I'm tired now."

We'd reached the bottom of the hill. "Would you like to ride Ben the rest of the way?"

"I used to be a fine horsewoman. Oh yes, I'd ride my horse all over these hills. I had a green velvet riding habit. Do you know about the staircase?"

The way she had of jumping from one subject to another certainly kept you alert, I decided. "At the church? Yes."

"They patterned that church after the Sainte-Chapelle, in Paris. They say it's the only Gothic church west of the Mississippi. I kept asking that architect, 'What about the staircase?' But he wouldn't listen to me. Threw me out. What did I know, an old Protestant lady? When I tried to tell the nuns—well, they never listen to what I say at all. Then when the builders left, the nuns scolded me for not telling them. And Bishop Lamy is so upset with Mother Magdalena about it. Those two don't get on too well. Mother Magdalena gets bossy and uppity. He's kinder in the heart."

I told her then about Elinora, and how my father had been paid to bring her here.

"Oh, he has a great fondness for that grandniece, the Bishop. She's his niece's child. So do you like Santa Fe, dearie?"

"I don't know it yet."

"Oh, it's a land of fancy. And a land of stark truth. The trick is to figure out when it is being which."

"Yes, ma'am."

"Sometimes everything seems prickly and sharp. And when it is not sticking you with its stark truth, it is enchanting you. There is enchantment, magic, everywhere. You must be careful of it. Did you know that Jesse James was here last night?"

I stared at her. Was she in or out of her head now? Her blue gaze was becalmed, peaceful. "He comes here sometimes to hide. Up in the fort." She pointed to where we'd just come from. "I never know when he'll come, but he and I get along. He's a nice young man. About the age my Robert would be now. His family was badly treated in the war, did you know that?"

"I come from Missouri," I said. "I know all about Jesse James." I felt very possessive of him, too. After all, he was ours in Missouri. What right did she have to lay claim to him here in New Mexico?

"He can't help doing what he's doing," she said. "He told me how the Pinkerton men blew up his house in Missouri and killed his young stepbrother."

I stared at her. Not many people outside Missouri knew that.

"He robs and steals to get back at authority. I wish I had a way of getting back at authority. Don't you?"

I thought of the plantation my father had lost. Of General Sherman's authority. *What kind of a girl would I be if we still had that plantation?* I'd often wondered. "Yes," I said.

"Whenever Jesse comes through, he hides out up there in the fort. I have other friends there, too. Maybe someday you'll meet them."

"If you're Protestant, why do you live at a Catholic convent?" I asked.

"They care for me. No one else will. But of course, I have paid my way. I gave a right-smart parcel of money to help build that cathedral. Which is why I was so annoyed when they didn't do the staircase right. They must find a builder to do it right. I keep telling them."

"There are plenty of missionaries and churches about."

"Not in Santa Fe, and I want to stay in Santa Fe. With Robert. In spite of all their mumbo jumbo, they're good people at Our Lady of Light. They just overdo the rules. And so I break them. They assign one of the girls to come with me every day. But the lily-livered little brats don't want anything to do with me. So if I want to visit Robert or Delvina, I have to go alone."

"Who's Delvina?"

"Why, she's my other friend up at the fort," she said, as if she'd already told me and I hadn't been paying mind. "She lives up there. I bring her food and extra blankets. She's darling. You'll have to meet her. She's to have a baby."

"She lives up there?"

"Of course! She has a husband, but he's meaner than a hornet. Strikes her. She can't go home. She's afraid he'll kill her. And the baby, too, when it comes. Last night Jesse James gave her a twenty-dollar gold piece. But you mustn't tell anybody any of this. You hear?"

"I hear," I said. *Crazy,* I thought. *Crazier than a hooty owl. Plain out of her head. Jesse James, indeed! Why, everybody knows Jesse James is up Missouri way, when he isn't hiding out in Kansas, Minnesota, or even Kentucky or Tennessee.* It was a game to keep track of his doings in Independence. All the girls in school dreamed of seeing him. Some lied and said they did. Rhoda Markus swore she'd seen him and his brother, Frank, eating over a small fire behind a cooperage at the end of town one day. Said they took their hats off to her.

We all prayed Jesse would rob the local bank. We collected reward posters. Hadn't my friend Cassie given me her best one?

Hadn't my own mama spoken herself with the Pinkerton men when they'd come around asking questions right after Annie Ralston of Independence ran off and married Jesse's brother, Frank? Because Mama knew the Ralstons.

No question about it. Jesse James was as much a hero to young people in Independence as he was a plague to their elders. But Jesse here? Wouldn't that be a hoot on the girls in Independence!

"And then there's Lozen." Mrs. Lacey was prattling on. "She comes by the fort sometimes, too."

"Lozen?"

"Yes, she's an Apache woman. Sister of the great war chief Victorio. He's trying to keep the Apache people free and alive. The Apaches have always been at war with Mexico. Sometimes she comes into New Mexico, to the fort to rest and pray and get strong."

I told her yes. I believed her. I agreed with everything she said. I acted interested, which I was. But they were fairy tales. I knew that. And my time for believing in fairy tales was over. I must get her back to the convent.

All the way home she talked, switching between the past and the present. I couldn't keep up with her. Inside my head I was pondering what I was going to tell Mother Magdalena about running off, and hoping that bringing this woman home—this daft woman who thought she knew Jesse James and the sister of an Apache chief—would redeem me.

6

❖

"RULE NUMBER ONE," Mother Magdalena declared firmly, "we do not leave the grounds without permission. Our girls do not roam the streets of Santa Fe."

"But most of the girls go home at night," I reasoned. "How do they get there?" I knew I was pushing it, but Uncle William had always said that when you are caught in the wrong, you must seize the argument by the tail and act with righteous indignation. "It rocks people off their feet," he said.

Mother Magdalena was not rocked.

Loudly she rapped her desk with a ruler. "You are sharp-tongued. A bold little piece, miss. We are trying to give you every leverage because you just lost your mother, but impudence is never tolerated at Our Lady of Light. We, here, encourage humility and ladylike behavior. Like the Virgin Mary." She pointed to the statue behind her desk. The Virgin had a snake at her feet, and she was stepping on it. That didn't look very humble or ladylike to me.

"Just where did you think you were going when you rode out the gate this morning?"

"To fetch *una madre,*" I lied.

"Her name is Mrs. Lacey."

"Ramona called her *una madre.* Ramona told me she was missing. So I rode in the direction Ramona gave me."

"You know Spanish, then?"

"No, ma'am."

"No, *Mother,*" she insisted.

She was a very tall woman. And her pointed wimple gave her more height. Her complexion was normally red. But when she became angry, it became even redder. And her blue eyes blazed. In my short time here I'd already learned that the girls were terrified of getting the rough side of her tongue. But she did not frighten me. "I can't call you *Mother,*" I told her, "because you aren't my mother."

"In the True Faith it is a symbolic term."

"I'm not of the True Faith. I mean no disrespect, but if it's all the same to you, I'll call you *ma'am.* No, ma'am, I don't know Spanish other than a few words. But I took Ramona's meaning."

She was too taken aback to know for a minute what to say. And I felt a small bubble of triumph inside me. Uncle William was right.

"You may not be of the True Faith, which only means that we must pray for your soul," she said, "but you are under my jurisdiction. In view of the fact that you just lost your mother, I shall not insist you use that term for me. But I will not tolerate impudence! I assume that impudence is frowned upon by Methodists as with Catholics?"

"Yes, ma'am."

"Very well. Nor will I tolerate disobedience. In the school you attended in Independence, were you allowed to leave the grounds whenever you chose?"

"No, ma'am."

"Then obedience is the same in Missouri as it is in Santa Fe, I assume."

I allowed that it was, while I tried to figure out how to make her assign me to Mrs. Lacey every day on her trip to the cemetery.

Uncle William had always said if you want something from someone, make them think you don't want it.

"Very well, then I believe you knew you were doing wrong this morning. And wrong must be punished. Now, I have several thoughts on the matter. First, I can take away your horse."

I felt my face go white. But somehow I managed not to let my fear show. People preyed on your fears. Something else Uncle William once told me.

"I can assign you special chores. Chores the girls consider most onerous."

"Please don't assign me to Crazy Lacey," I begged. "She's a daft old lady. She talks about meeting Jesse James. Everybody knows Jesse James doesn't come down this way. And she leaves a lantern at her son's grave because he was afraid of the dark. Mind you, I think she's sweet, ma'am, but sure as a tarantula has long legs, she's cracked in the dome."

"Don't be disrespectful, Elizabeth. Mrs. Lacey is a dear woman who has been a friend to this church and convent, though she is not of the True Faith. We shall all be old someday, Lord willing. And as such we, too, will deserve respect."

"But then why are you going to hang a bag of asafetida around her neck to punish her?"

She looked at me sharply. "Who said that?"

"She did."

"Asafetida prevents croup and colds. She is prone to such.

And if I ever put a bag of it around her neck, it is not for punishment. The woman gets mixed up in her head sometimes. Surely you know that by now."

"Yes, ma'am," I said meekly. "But—"

She cut me off. "Enough!" She raised her hand to silence me, and I fell silent, pouting to please her. "Henceforth, as long as you are with us and as long as the good Lord allows Mrs. Lacey to live amongst us, she is your responsibility."

"Ma'am?" I can pretend stupidity with the best of them. I learned that back in Independence, in Miss Cannon's fifth grade. Mother Magdalena had nothing on Miss Cannon, who terrorized her class with a ruler she wielded like a saber.

"Every day, after your lessons are completed, you will accompany Mrs. Lacey to Fort Marcy so she can bring flowers to her son's grave."

"Ma'am, that place is creepy. Please, I'll take any other punishment."

"You have proved yourself adept with her, Elizabeth. She told me she likes you."

"But she wants to bring food for her dead son." Of course, I knew who the food was for.

"The food is not for her dead son, Elizabeth," she said sadly. "It is for Delvina."

"Ma'am? You *know* about Delvina?"

She smiled, and I had to admit that her face softened in the most disarming way. "There is not much I do not know around here, Elizabeth. You might make a note of that for future reference."

"But then, if you don't mind my asking, ma'am, why don't you do something about Delvina?"

"And what would you suggest we do, Elizabeth?"

"Why, bring her here. Give her a place."

"Impossible. And if I must answer to you, it is impossible because her husband is a known brigand hereabouts. Your Jesse James from Missouri is a lesser angel compared to him. He is, God help him, a drunkard, a wife-beater, a thief, and worse. If he knew she was here, our safety would be threatened. I cannot endanger my girls. So, you will keep your own good counsel about Delvina. Tell no one. Or I will have to forbid Mrs. Lacey from visiting her son's grave. Is that clear?"

"Yes, ma'am." It wasn't, of course. How she, who was supposed to be of the True Faith, could allow a woman expecting a child to live in an abandoned fort was beyond my understanding. I knew what my own mama would do about the problem, all right.

"There are one or two more things before you go," she was saying.

I sighed wearily.

"Henceforth, if you do not wish me to take your horse, you will leave the grounds only to take Mrs. Lacey to the graveyard. And then, only when you sign out. And as of today, you will wear the purple school uniform. Girls who are seen in that on the streets are known to be from this school, and everyone respects them. You will attend regular classes, mass every morning, and the novena we are making to Saint Joseph for the staircase."

"Novena? Isn't mass enough? I don't even understand the mass. All that Latin."

"The novena is very important to us here, and, as part of the school, should be important to you, too. We need a staircase to the choir loft."

"I know. Mrs. Lacey told me."

She gave me a queer look. "I'm not surprised. She is downright crazed on the subject. Even gave us more money, after her first contribution to the church, to find a good carpenter to build one. Says she is doing it for Robert, her son. She has some strange notion that Robert won't rest in peace until the church is completed. And to her that means the staircase. And she's not even Catholic!"

Then why don't you get a carpenter, I wanted to say. But, of course, I didn't.

"It is a major crisis at the moment, that staircase. We hoped our first Christmas in the new chapel would be celebrated in a fashion after the Bishop's beloved Sainte-Chapelle, in Paris. We have exhausted every other hope. Our last resort is a novena to Saint Joseph."

I was not expected to reply, thank heavens. Not being of the True Faith, I thought simply that she was living in a dream world. I was dismissed then, so she informed me. I was to go right to classes. And as part of my punishment it was henceforth my duty to bring Mrs. Lacey's meals to her room, also.

"She drinks only goat's milk. She will ask you to sneak coffee out of the kitchen for her. She is inordinately fond of coffee. But under no circumstances are you to do so. She has neuralgia. Sister Roberta is in charge of the infirmary, and you are to inform her should the neuralgia act up. She will give you a pillow filled with hops and heated in the oven."

"Yes, ma'am." I started to leave. At the door, I turned. "Ma'am? Can I ride Ben when I take Mrs. Lacey to Fort Marcy? Sometimes she gets tired and—"

"Yes, yes." She waved me off, and her attention was then on some papers on her desk. She was finished with me. I no longer existed. I was no more than a dust mote in her eye. I closed the door and went down the hall to my first class, which was French. *Why French,* I thought, *when I need to know Spanish?*

I'd won, hadn't I? Wouldn't Uncle William be proud of me? Hadn't I taken the argument by the tail and acted with righteous indignation? She wasn't taking away Ben. I'd outsmarted her by making her think the worst thing in the world she could do to me was to make me take Mrs. Lacey to Fort Marcy every day. When I didn't mind at all. Why, she'd given me permission to take Ben, and everything.

Except for wearing the purple uniform and going to mass and her stupid novena every day, I had bested her. Even Uncle William would say so.

Then why did I feel as if the woman had seen into my soul? In that moment as I went down the hall to class, I recollected the Arapaho who had walked into our camp that night on the Trail, and how he had looked at me, and what he had said about me. Funny, I hadn't thought of him since then. Something in Mother Magdalena's eyes had reminded me of him.

I felt a stab of hunger and remembered I hadn't had much breakfast. Either that, or it was a small bubble of triumph inside me bursting into a thousand pieces.

7

MOTHER MAGDALENA'S RULE NUMBER ONE, not leaving the grounds without permission, was easy. After all, I had permission to leave every day in order to take Mrs. Lacey to the cemetery.

I wore the school uniform, dreadful purple thing, hanging to my feet under my heavy shawl. And people were respectful to me on the street. Or maybe it was being with Mrs. Lacey. She knew everybody. We walked through town—I, leading Ben—and people waved to her. Men doffed their sombreros. We couldn't get to the end of town without being stopped by at least five people inquiring after her or telling about their troubles. She was interested in everybody's child, everybody's sick mother, every new family that came in on the Santa Fe Trail.

She had a small silk bag tied to her waist inside her warm shawl. In it were coins. She gave them out to many who spoke with her. In another silk bag, she kept candy. Some were peppermints, some licorice, and some were candy hearts. She gave these out to the little Mexican and Indian children playing *kanute* on the streets. It was a kind of shell game.

It took us a very long time to get through town.

We stopped at the marketplace. I loved the marketplace, with its booths piled high with red and blue corn, its hanging peppers, its melons, chamois coats, hand-carved chests, Indian pottery, Mexican turquoise jewelry, colorful shawls, and every other thing under the sun.

I loved the sleepy burros that stood waiting for their masters to sell their wares. I stared at the dark-eyed *señoritas* smoking *cigarillos* in the doorways. Elinora had told me they wore no underwear. They didn't wear petticoats, I could see that. Or corsets or long sleeves. Their skirts reached just above their ankles. Never had I seen women so boldly dressed.

Mrs. Lacey bought me a pair of Indian moccasins and candy that looked like shelled corn. I protested. "You are my friend," she said. And I stopped protesting, knowing it was enough.

We walked past the Governor's Palace on Central Plaza. At the end of the building was a large grillwork door. Mrs. Lacey knew the prisoner behind that door. She called him Billy the Kid. He came to the grillwork to say hello to her. He was young and sassy. She chatted with him awhile and told him how proud she was of the part he'd taken with the Regulators in the Lincoln County War. "Nobody appreciated what you people did," she told him.

He thanked her. She gave him some candy, and we went on. "He's New Mexico's Jesse James," she said. "He'll escape from prison, don't worry."

"He can't be Billy the Kid," I said, "or we would have heard he was here." Surely the gossipy girls at school would have mentioned it.

"Oh, I call him Billy. He likes it and goes along with it. It enlivens his days."

Once I got her up the hill to Fort Marcy, the miseries would come upon me. The grave site, the whole cemetery, made me uneasy. Not because the dead were there. Not because some of their bones were coming to the surface. But because I wished Mama were here, and I thought of her lonely grave covered over with stones on the prairie. And my spirit would be so spent that I wanted to stand there and howl out my misery like a wolf.

Each day I'd look for her, but so far I hadn't seen Delvina.

"Where is she?" I asked Mrs. Lacey on the third visit to the cemetery.

"She's here."

"But where?"

"She's not ready for you to see her yet. There are really a lot of people here."

"A lot?" I looked around at the deserted fort with its crumbling walls through which the wind whistled. I felt eyes watching me.

"Some are very old gods," she explained patiently, while she lit the lantern in the little stone cubicle next to her son's grave. "Some are ghosts, like Governor Perez. He was beheaded by the Pueblo Indians forty years ago. And some are alive. Like Delvina and Lozen. It's a wonderful place to hide."

I looked into her eyes and saw she was having one of her "moments." So I got on Ben and rode off to the edges of Fort Marcy, where there were cedar and Russian olive trees. The afternoon sun was warm, but this first week in November there was snow on top of the Sangre de Cristos in the east. I saw sheep grazing on distant mesas. I knew dark would come quickly. It was my job to get Mrs. Lacey home before dark.

Already the sun was getting itself ready to drop behind the Jemez Mountains in the west.

I could smell the smoke of the piñon logs, rising in the air from fireplaces in town. Dusk was my worst time for the miseries. I felt my losses stand out sharply inside me. I felt my soul like the landscape around me, its green places all gone, its pain jutting out, exposed and unprotected, like the bare bones in the cemetery. Once back at the academy the hustle and bustle; the chatter of the five girls who boarded, Lucy and Consuello, Winona, Rosalyn, and Elinora; the sounds and smells from the kitchen, where supper was being prepared, would distract me. So I wanted to get back, away from here.

Still, I would wait a bit and give Mrs. Lacey her time. I knew she had prayers to say, that in still another sack she had food for Delvina, that before we departed she must set it out and leave it. So I devoted myself to Ben and the view. But I still felt eyes on me.

THAT FIRST WEEK at the academy I was so confused I felt like a mule in a mud hut. Every which way I turned I broke some rule.

The convent was like a mirage in the desert. Everything looked calm and inviting and peaceful and elegant. But none of those qualities were there. The nuns never raised their voices, but their sad disapproval was damnation in whispers. Sin was everywhere, in everything I did.

During the week when all the girls were present, to speak at meals was a sin. You had to be quiet, while a nun read from some book of lessons that told about saints undergoing whippings and being eaten by lions, and having their heads cut off to preserve their souls.

To swear was a sin, and of course I'd learned to swear from Uncle William. To eat meat on Friday was a sin. On Friday you ate fish. And all I could think of was Fridays on the Trail, when we were so happy to bag an antelope or a rabbit.

To have pride was a sin. Humility was everything, though all the girls preened and boasted and glowed when they got praise from the nuns. To have impure thoughts was a sin. I'd been having them for two years already. Chastity was the biggest prize of all, the one you fought for every day in a battle with yourself. Some girls prayed to be attacked on the streets on the way home so they could fight off their attacker and be stabbed and die for their chastity.

These same girls spoke constantly of the boys school "over the fence," behind ours. And when they spoke of it they giggled and whispered. The fence was built of adobelike material, with a grillwork gate between the properties. By some hapless bit of planning—likely the kind that had made the carpenter forget the staircase in the chapel—there was a grotto with the Virgin in it in the middle of the fence. My first two days at the convent I'd learned that boys from school dropped over the fence and met girls behind the statue of the Virgin. It was a risky business, and only the brave dared it.

In the name of chastity the girls who boarded at the convent, the five besides me, all bathed in their undergarments. I tried it once. All it led to was my chemise and pantalets sticking to me, and I couldn't figure out how to get clean, and then I was left with dripping undergarments.

To covet what somebody else had was a sin. Yet the girls were jealous if someone got a new ribbon or special attention or praise from a nun. And they all discovered Ben, of course. And were already begging for rides on him. Lying was a sin, but I told Mother Magdalena that Ben had a penchant for kicking strangers who came too close and for tossing off girls he didn't know. Just ask Elinora.

Worst of all, to be angry with God was a sin. And I thought of my daddy, and how he hadn't prayed since he lost his arm in the war.

Of course, to dishonor your parents was very bad. This nearly put me into a state of apoplexy. I was supposed to pray for Daddy every day—to love him, to forgive him for walking off without even saying good-bye.

The nuns told us that we should all keep our hearts open to see if we had a calling. That the highest destiny for a young girl was to become a bride of Christ.

Each May they crowned the Virgin Mary. All the girls hoped to be the one to crown, come May, because they would get to wear a bridal gown and veil. They wanted to practice, because many expected to wed by the time they reached sixteen and to have many babies.

The nuns told us that if the babies died, we mustn't mourn, because we were creating souls for heaven. But if they died before baptism, they would not go to heaven, but to someplace called Limbo. They would never see God.

This bothered me more than bathing in my undergarments. Why should a little baby be suspended forever in someplace called Limbo? Why would God not want to see it?

If they had a cold or cramps, or had to do an onerous chore, they were told to "offer it up" for the "poor souls." I thought they were talking about the poor on the streets until I understood it was the poor souls who were burning for their sins in purgatory. In church the priest was always praying for the "intestines of the Holy Father" in Rome. I thought the poor man had gout of the stomach until Elinora told me it was *intentions,* not *intestines.*

The girls were always sacrificing, giving up sugar in their coffee, meat when they didn't have to, butter or jam on their bread. I, on the other hand, was always hungry. They would give me dirty looks at the table when I took a second helping. I didn't care. I heaped butter on my bread, right in front of them.

Some of the Sisters got up in the middle of the night, got out of cold beds, to go into the chapel and pray. "It's so that God won't be lonely," Elinora explained to me.

I didn't see how God could be lonely. Didn't He have the whole world He created? If He was lonely, why didn't He take some of those babies from Limbo? I didn't understand anything about these people. They set up barricades for themselves, made rules it was impossible to live by, then enjoyed their guilt. I'd understood that Arapaho Indian better.

Didn't God have my mother? How could he be lonely?

How I longed for the straight, simple, clean lines and the uncluttered faith of the Methodist church in Independence. All this talk of blood and martyrdom and eating flesh and agony. It was just too much, is all.

OF COURSE, THERE were nice things, too. Besides the music. But the music! When Elinora did her solo singing "Panis Angelicus," I thought someone was wringing out my soul. No wonder these girls were always swooning.

Some of their prayers had phrases that gripped me and held me in their jaws, like one of my cats held a mouse. "They have numbered all my bones" was one phrase. I thought how fitting it was, Christ saying that about himself. Was it blasphemous, I wondered, to feel akin to it at times? To feel that you were so hurt, so exposed, so haunted, that they could number all your bones?

"Blessed be God in His angels and in His saints," they prayed. And I thought, yes, we would say "and His angels" or "with His angels." But the way they said it, though it defied all proper English, was right, I decided. In His angels. And in His saints.

BY THE END OF the first week, I learned, too, that of all fifty-one girls at the school, I was the only one not of the True Faith. And that practically all of them were praying for visions.

"Like the Indians have?" I asked Elinora.

She said no, the girls were praying for a vision of the Virgin Mary. "Watch in church," she told me. "Sometimes you will see a girl kneeling there, her eyes all glazed over, not blinking at all, very still and enraptured."

"Does that mean she's having a vision?" I asked.

"No," Elinora said. "That means she's faking it." Elinora was getting bitter because her granduncle, the Bishop, was still not back from his trip, to make a fuss over her. "They all fake it. They lie about seeing the Virgin," she said.

I understood, then. It was like the girls at home in Independence lied about seeing Jesse James.

FRENCH WAS NOT EASY.

For one thing, all the girls were ahead of me. The language spilled off their tongues. Sister Roberta taught French. She was a very large woman. Yet her weight seemed to be all strength, not flab. She kept fish in large tanks in her classroom, and she could lift and move those tanks of water like they were pillows. She had a sallow-complected round face and a lot of hair above her upper lip. But somewhere in her bulky frame, under all those black clothes and behind that wimple that framed her face, was a young mischievous girl trying to get out. I sensed it by the way she cracked jokes and her eyes twinkled. I liked her on first sight.

The other girls made fun of her and whispered in class. This day they whispered about the novena to Saint Joseph. Tonight was the seventh night for it. Every night for a week now we'd gone to the chapel, and after the usual evening prayers, the priest conducted the novena.

I was getting accustomed to the incense, the Latin, the chanting responses to the prayers. Evening prayers in the chapel were like an oasis in the confusion of the school. First, the day students were gone and there were only a few of us and the nuns. Second, the whole business gave me a sense of peace. Or at least time to study on things and sort them out.

It was the only time I really allowed myself to think about Mama.

Oh, she came to me during the day, especially at the cemetery. I would think, "I'll have to remember to tell Mama this." Or, "Mama won't like this; wait until she finds out."

And then I would remember there would be no more telling her anything. No more waiting until she found out things. She would never again find out. But most painful was the blankness that came after minding that she was gone forever. That was when I wanted to howl like a wolf. I did not understand *forever* in the same sentence as Mama being gone. So I would push the thought of her from my mind. Until evening services.

Then she came at me. I couldn't hold her off anymore. She came at me with the full force of a dust storm. I was helpless as a tumbleweed in the dust storm she created. She was in my nostrils, with the memory of the lavender she used. She was in my ears, telling me to never help my father unless he asked for help, because he had to feel independent with one arm.

I'd sit there benumbed with her swirling around me in the middle of the smell of incense and the grip of the music. I had held her off all day, and now I was too weary. And it did not matter, because here I could let the tears flow and nobody cared. Some girl was crying all the time, caught in a fit of romantic holiness.

It went together, the mumbo jumbo of the Latin, the nothingness that my mother had become, and the fact that the nuns and the girls expected that there would somehow magically appear, behind the last pew in the chapel, a staircase. Because they prayed to Saint Joseph.

I felt cheated, because I could not believe this. I wished I could. I knew that if I could just believe, I would understand Mama's death, too. And the way my father had left me.

I'd sit there and wish I could believe in something. Maybe just in my father.

FOUR NUNS RAN THE SCHOOL—Mother Magdalena, Sister Catherine, Sister Hilaria, and Sister Roberta. Sister Roberta ran the infirmary, taught French, nursed the sick, and sometimes helped Ramona in the kitchen. I had to go to the infirmary to fetch medicine for Mrs. Lacey. It was a small, many-windowed room that caught the light of the morning and the afternoon sun. All around on the wide windowsills, Sister Roberta grew her special plants, and at one end was a potbellied stove to keep them warm. In the infirmary she rolled her long, loose black sleeves up above the elbows. She wore boots because the brick floor was often wet from watering her plants. She tucked her skirts up in and around her belt, so I could see she had legs.

Also, she smoked.

She smoked a pipe. "Only in here," she said. "The fragrance is good for the plants." And she winked at me.

It came to me, then. She was the one who'd carried me upstairs on my first night here, when I'd smelled Daddy's tobacco and thought he'd grown another arm.

On top of the potbellied stove, she also kept a pot of coffee boiling at all times. She'd put Mrs. Lacey's medicine in a small basket. Next to it she'd put a mug of coffee, sweet, with milk and a bit of nutmeg. The first time she did this I'd given her a questioning glance and she'd smiled and shaken a finger at me. "God forgives disobedience," she said, "when the act helps someone in need."

I was soon to discover that Sister Roberta had her own ten commandments.

After that I think I would have died for her. And then, at the end of my first week in school, she made me remain after the others in French class.

"Your French is deplorable," she said.

I summoned the mettle to suffer a scolding, but instead she smiled. "Personally, I don't see why these girls have to learn French. It's the Bishop. Anything French is dear to him."

"I just can't seem to learn it, Sister," I said.

"We will teach you."

"I don't think I'll be here long enough to learn."

"Oh? I hope you don't leave too soon. I'd like you to come along with me to the river. I need to pick some O-pshaw. My supply is running low."

I said I would likely be here. At least for a while.

"Aren't you going to ask what O-pshaw is?" she asked.

"What is it, Sister?"

"A Mexican cure-all. They have many such remedies. Half magic and half tradition. I don't believe in it as much as some of these girls do. Its curative powers are in the belief it fosters. Like so many things you will find they use around here."

I met her calm, unblinking gaze. Was she speaking of the novena to Saint Joseph?

"I'd love to go with you, Sister."

"I also have to fetch more bark from the wild chokecherry tree. And make some cough syrup with honey for Bishop Lamy. He's due home in a week. He always returns home from his trips with a cough. Tell me, where are you going when you leave here?"

"I beg your pardon?"

"You said you were leaving. What are your plans?"

I stared up at her. Her eyes looked as if she was about to burst into laughter any minute. "I don't know," I said. "I only know I can't stay here. Maybe I'll write to my uncle William and ask him if I can come back to Independence."

"Is he the one who taught you to swear?"

"Yes, Sister. How did you know?"

"I met your uncle William once."

"You did?"

"We Sisters come from Kentucky, you know. Before you were born. Bishop Lamy summoned us here to start the school. We came by paddle wheeler up the Mississippi. Then by wagon from St. Louis. By the time we got to Independence, three of us were taken with the cholera, myself included. We had to stay there awhile. We lost Mother Matilda to the cholera. Your uncle saw to it that we were put up in the best lodging, and he kept us supplied with everything we needed."

I beamed. "That sounds like Uncle William."

"What do you plan on doing when he writes that you should return? Living at Fort Bent?"

"I hadn't thought on it," I said.

"Your grandfather was just starting to build the new Fort Bent when we came through. I always wanted to see it. If I were a man, I'd be a fur trapper. What about you?"

"I'd join Jesse James."

She smiled again. "Do you think you could stay with us until Delvina has her baby?"

"You know about Delvina?"

"We all do. How do you think Mrs. Lacey gets food from the kitchen to take to her? We'll have to be sending her heavier blankets soon. Nights get very cold by mid-November."

"I don't understand, Sister. How can people who believe Saint Joseph will bring them a staircase leave her up there? Who will deliver her baby?"

"Saint Joseph will give us a staircase. And we will bring her here. That's why I want you to stay. I need to be kept apprised of her situation. As she nears her time, we must bring her here."

"Mother Magdalena won't allow it."

"Even Mother Magdalena isn't that heartless. Will you find out from her when she is expecting her lying-in?"

"I haven't even met her yet."

"You will. Soon. Maybe tomorrow. Promise me you will. And promise me you will stay until she has the child."

Where else would I go? I promised.

8

✤

BY SATURDAY I HAD STAKED out my claim in the room I shared with Elinora. My poster of Jesse James that Cassie had given me, I pasted on the wall over my bed. It was about as fine a poster as could be. It offered five thousand dollars for the capture of Jesse W. James "in perpetration of the robbery last aforesaid."

Next to both of our beds, which were against opposite walls, were little shelves. On hers Elinora had a statue of the Virgin. On mine was my chamois sack that Daddy had given me. It had once held his Bull Durham tobacco and still carried the fragrance. In it was an agate marble I'd won in a game in the schoolyard in Independence, a piece of Mama's hair in a small locket that she'd given me just before she died, and three horsehairs wrapped around an eagle feather I'd found on the trail. It was my good-luck charm. Everybody had to have one.

"You shouldn't have that drunken heathen's picture on your wall." Elinora stood in the doorway.

"He isn't a drunk. He never drinks anything stronger than beer."

"You know that, I suppose."

"Yes." I was kneeling on my bed, straightening the poster. "I also know that he believes in out-of-body travel, that he was named after his mother's brother who committed suicide, that he doesn't swear in front of ladies, that he married his first cousin, and that his mother had her arm blown off when Pinkerton men attacked her home. Just like my father had his blown off in the war."

"And all that makes him a hero, I suppose."

"In Missouri he's one."

"Missouri is a robber state. Mother Magdalena said so. She said the Chicago newspapers reported that in no state but Missouri would the James brothers be tolerated for so many years."

"You come from Missouri."

"Why do you think I wanted to leave? Anyway, I come from St. Louis, where people are civilized. You ought to have a statue of the Virgin on your shelf. Or at least of Saint Joseph."

"I'm sick to the teeth of Saint Joseph already."

"Hush!" Elinora closed the door and stepped into the room. "Tonight is the eighth night of the novena. You'll hex it by being blasphemous."

"You talk of Saint Joseph like he had sorcerer's powers."

"Will you hush! Oh, why did they ever put me in the room with you! A heretic!"

"I was asking myself the same question, Elinora. Why did they ever put me in the room with a ninny who parrots everything the nuns say? And doesn't have an opinion of her own."

"I have opinions." She paced, hands clasped behind her

back. Her thick glasses gave her eyes the look of a toad's. "And I'm not as much of a ninny as you think. As a matter of fact, I came up to ask you if you wanted to go on a lark with me."

"A lark?"

"You don't know what a lark is?"

"Well, in Independence it could mean sneaking downtown to stand outside the grog shops at night to see the hurdy-gurdy girls. But I'm sure in St. Louis it consists of putting your elbows on the dinner table."

"You needn't be so superior. I've sneaked out at night twice this week already."

I stared at her hard; she stared right back. "You snore at night. I hear it all night long."

"Funny, you're sleeping pretty deeply when I do it."

I nodded, bested. "Where do you go?"

"With some other girls. To meet friends from the boys school, by the grotto. I've already met one nice young man and plan to meet him again. Are you going to tell?"

"No," I said. "But if your uncle finds out, he'll be crushed."

"He won't find out. Not unless you tell. It's harmless. The worst we do is smoke a *cigarillo*. Now, do you want to come with me tonight or not?"

"I have no interest in meeting boys at the grotto."

"Not there. I'm going to visit someone who can give me advice. I need some good advice right now."

"Then why don't you ask Mother Magdalena? You know you're her pet."

"Only because I'm the Bishop's grandniece. I know that, too. It's advice that regards my future. And I don't trust her."

"Who is going to give you this advice, then?"

Elinora gave a secret smile. "Come with me, and you'll see. And you might even have some fun in the bargain."

I NEVER WOULD HAVE expected it of droopy-drawers Elinora. First, that she would want to disobey the rules, and second, that she would ask me to accompany her.

She was the most unlikely of confederates. The only reason I could think that she chose me was that none of the other namby-pamby girls who boarded would go with her. They would only risk sneaking out to meet with boys. Besides, I was curious. What advice did Miss Know-It-All need about her future? And from whom?

She had our escape all planned. After the eighth night of the novena, after we girls who boarded were allowed into the kitchen for a warm cup of cocoa and were then sent upstairs to bed and the convent got quiet, we two sneaked out.

It was not as difficult as it sounds, because the nuns were back in the chapel, adding more prayers to Saint Joseph's list, and we simply walked out.

Elinora had a lantern, we both wore moccasins to dull our footfalls, and the door by which we left was in the kitchen. Unlocked. Elinora had arranged all nighttime adventures with Ramona, who, as it turned out, had a special request for the Bishop when he came. Everybody gained. Ramona, the girls who sneaked out, and certainly Elinora.

Ramona wanted a new cast-iron stove in the kitchen. The one she presently used smoked unmercifully, and Elinora had promised her that she would speak to her uncle about it. Of course, not even Ramona would enter into such a conspiracy if she knew the girls met with boys at night. They told her they simply wanted to sit in the garden and watch the stars.

This night Elinora lied to her again. She told Ramona we were going to check on Doña Elenita, a friend of Mrs. Lacey's, and that Mrs. Lacey was not able to sleep until she heard that this friend's baby's fever had broken. We would be only an hour. Ramona was inordinately fond of Mrs. Lacey. She was always baking special delicacies for her. And she had instructed her husband, Gregorio, who was also the gardener, to let us out the front gate and in an hour be waiting to let us back in.

What we were really doing was paying a visit to Dolores la Penca. She lived on Agua Fria Road.

She was a good witch.

Consuello, one of the night boarders at the school, had told us about Dolores. And explained to us the difference between *curanderas,* good witches, and *brujas,* bad witches.

Consuello had told us of Dolores la Penca's reputation of healing and relieving suffering and illness. And how she had special powers to predict the future.

Elinora had boned up on Dolores, and on other witches in Santa Fe. I thought I might ask this woman if I would ever hear from my father again. So we set off in the bone-chilling November evening. In a small basket, Elinora had some tortillas left over from supper, and cooked dried chokecherries. Ramona sent it along for Doña Elenita. We, of course, would give it as an offering to Dolores, the good witch.

I held our lantern as we stole through the streets. At first I was very frightened. What I saw bore no resemblance at all to Santa Fe in the daytime. The people looked different, sinister. The young *señoritas* had let their hair down and it flowed on their backs like horses' manes. They wore pearl and amber combs high in their hair. Their skirts were bright red. Men wore scarlet sashes and tight pants and polished boots. Their outfits gleamed with silver, and they all seemed possessed by a quality of languorous confidence.

It was the light, I decided. The brightness of day was gone, with all its brutal truth. A special glow was thrown out onto the wooden walks from the saloons, from which drifted the music of guitars and mandolins. There was excitement in the air as we made our way through the throngs of people. I pressed closer to Elinora, who seemed to know her way.

We turned down a side lane, and the street was filled with menacing shadows. Our small lantern gave scant light. Up ahead a single window glowed with light. "That's it," Elinora said.

She did have brass, I decided.

"Consuello said this is the oldest house in Santa Fe," Elinora told me as we walked up the lane. "Another witch lives here with Dolores, but she isn't often home. I suspect that on a night such as this she is out riding her fireball. New Mexico's witches ride fireballs instead of brooms, you know."

I stared at her. "You believe that?"

"I don't dare not believe it. Any more than I dare not believe that they can cure a migraine headache by passing an egg across your forehead. Or cure a serious illness by hitting the person's shadow with a broom. Now, be careful what you say to Dolores. Call her ma'am, like you do Mother Magdalena. They require utmost respect. They can put hexes on people, too, you know. Whatever you do, just don't make the sign of the cross in her presence."

I nodded silently. And then, as we neared the house, a figure stepped out of the shadows. At first he seemed to be an old man, poorly clad in some rough cloak. Behind him stood a mule, and over the mule's back was a sack. "*Scusa,*" he said.

"Oh!" Elinora stepped closer to me, startled.

"Very sorry," the man said. As he stepped out of the shadows, I held up the lantern and saw he was not that old. Only his eyes were. His face was one minute young and the next like my father's, lined but not old. "I did not mean to frighten you. I heard you talking and thought I might ask."

"Ask what?"

I thought Elinora was being unnecessarily rude, but I kept a still tongue in my head.

The man searched her face with those old eyes of his, then looked at me and smiled, almost as if he recognized me. "I need some work," he said. "I am a carpenter. I am new to town and I need some work. My tools are in that sack." He pointed to the mule. "Do you young ladies perhaps know of someone who needs some building to be done?"

"Certainly not," Elinora said. "But I do know that no gentleman approaches young ladies on the street in Santa Fe. Especially when we are wearing the uniform of Our Lady of Light Academy!"

I pulled her aside. "Elinora, he said he's new to town," I protested. "How would he know our uniforms?"

"He's still no gentleman if he does not recognize young ladies of quality," she whispered.

I had a thought then. "What about the staircase in the chapel? It needs a builder."

"Nonsense," she whispered back savagely. "Can't you see he's dressed like a beggar? What would he know about building a staircase in such an elegant chapel?"

"We must be on our way," she said to the man. "I am sorry. Perhaps if you ask tomorrow in town."

He nodded solemnly. Then he gestured with his head to the witches' house. "Have a care in there."

"What?" Elinora asked indignantly.

"Don't believe everything you hear. There is only one magic." And he pointed to his chest. "The goodness of the heart."

"Come on, Lizzy." Elinora pulled my arm.

"Wait." I stood firm, and something compelled me to pay mind to this man. There was about him something familiar. I felt as if I knew him. It was the same way I felt about Sister Roberta. "Sir, are you hungry?" I asked.

He smiled. "It has been awhile since I have partaken of food. And my mule here could use some fodder."

"If you wait until we come out of this house, you can come back to the school with us. The nuns often feed hungry strangers."

"Lizzy!" Elinora's whisper was fierce. "What's wrong with you? Bring him back? We aren't even supposed to be out!"

"I don't wish to cause trouble," the man said.

"Then go, and leave us be!" Elinora grabbed my arm and pulled me in the direction of the gate to the witches' house. I looked over my shoulder to smile at the man, but he had disappeared into the shadows.

We went through the little gate and up the walk. A light burned beyond the windows. Firmly Elinora knocked. A silky youthful voice came from the other side of the iron grillwork door. "I will be there in a moment."

"Oh, one more thing," Elinora cautioned. "Don't look directly into her eyes. They know the art of the *ojo malo,* the evil eye. They can make you sick with a stare. She has been known to turn men into women. And women into coyotes."

The door opened.

The woman who stood there seemed too young to be a witch, although I must admit that night I could not fathom anybody's age. She wore a black skirt and a shawl. At first I thought the shawl was ragged. Then I saw it had strips of cloth sewn on it that dangled down, like wide fringe. And there were some designs on the strips; they looked to be Indian. And when she moved they appeared to be luminous in the lantern light.

"Ah, the little girls from the academy. Come in. Consuello told me to expect you this evening." She stepped aside, and hesitantly I followed Elinora through the door and quickly looked around.

The house seemed elegantly furnished, as far as rugs and silver plate and curios and polished wood, but it was overcluttered. From the rafters hung bundles of herbs. On the wide windowsills sat pots of plants. There was a cast-iron stove in the corner, the kind Ramona wanted for her kitchen. On it were cast-iron pots simmering with liquids that let off putrid smells.

"Come in, come in, sit down," Dolores said. She took the lantern from my hand, held it up before her, stared at it, and the candle within went out. I felt a chill. I followed Elinora to the hearth, where a fire burned. I sat on a settle next to Elinora. Dolores sat opposite us. I slid my eyes around again, looking for cats or brooms. I saw none, but in a moment I heard a rustling of feathers, then felt something fly past my head. I put my arms up to protect myself.

"That's only Sitting Bull," she said. And she laughed at our wide-eyed response. "Watch when he lights on something. There, doesn't he look like an Indian chief?"

The owl had taken hold of a wire rod on a table. He snuggled down into his feathers and eyed us steadily. I saw no resemblence to any Indian I ever knew, but Elinora said, "Yes, yes," as if she recognized the likeness.

"Now, tell me what you require," Dolores said.

Elinora sighed heavily. "First let me give you this." She handed over the small basket of food intended for Doña Elenita.

"An offering. Thank you. I see they teach you manners at the academy. Well, come now, it grows late. And I am sure you must soon be back."

"Yes." Elinora cast me a sideways look and plunged in. "Ma'am," she said, "I know you give advice. I need it badly. It concerns my future."

Outside the wind had picked up and rattled at the windows. Dolores gazed intently at Elinora, waiting.

"I think I have a calling," Elinora said. "As a matter of fact, I am sure of it. I want to become a nun. I need you to tell me if my calling is real."

More wind and rattling windows. For an instant all the candles flickered, and from the corner of my eye I saw Sitting Bull hop to another perch, closer to us than before. *That old man out there will be cold,* I found myself thinking crazily. *We must get him back to the convent. Maybe he can sleep in the barn tonight. I'll give some of Ben's food to his mule.*

For a moment or two the old man was all I could think of. I tried desperately to recall who he reminded me of, where I had seen him before. I closed my eyes, the better to see him again, gentle and asking for work. And admonishing us to "have a care in there." That there is only one magic, the goodness of the heart.

I knew in that moment a terrible need to take him back with us. It became more and more urgent and right in my mind as I sat there.

And then Elinora was shaking me. I jerked myself awake. I'd fallen asleep! Oh, I felt so embarrassed. The fire was low in the hearth. Dolores got up, bent over it, blew on it, and all at once it came to life with a crackling glow.

"We must leave, Elinora," I said. "It's late."

Sitting Bull's eyes were closed. I pulled Elinora to her feet. Dolores led us to the door.

"Be careful going home. And remember what I told you," she said to Elinora. Then she blew on Elinora's lantern and a light appeared on the candle.

What had she told her? I had dozed. Or had I? And then as the chill night air hit me I knew the truth. Dolores the witch had put me under a spell so I couldn't hear what had transpired between them. I hadn't even had a chance to ask her if I would hear from my father again. I felt cheated. I was angry as the door closed behind us, and the minute I could adjust my eyes to the darkness I looked for the man and his mule.

He was there in the shadows. Waiting.

9

❖

ELINORA ABIDED THE MAN and his mule only because she
was so tainted with vanity on the way back about what Dolores
had told her.

"I have a calling, Lizzy! She told me it was true! I have a
calling to be a nun! Oh, wait until I tell my uncle!"

The man and his mule followed a discreet distance behind
us. "You want to be a nun?" I was incredulous. "What about
your singing? I thought you wanted to be like Jenny Lind."

"I want to be a nun. I just wasn't sure if my calling was
true, before tonight. Now I know it is!" She did a little jig on
the wooden walk. "Oh, look, there's a crowd up ahead. What
do you suppose is going on?"

The crowd was assembling at the end of the Governor's
Palace, where the jail was. "I don't know," I said. But I had a
queer fear inside me. We had stopped to stare, and the old
man's voice came from behind us. "Perhaps it would be good
to travel on another street."

Elinora had forgotten he was with us. She stared up at
him. "Yes, let's walk one street over." So we went down a side

street to avoid trouble. I was surprised that Elinora had taken his advice, or even condescended to speak to him. At the same time, I had the feeling she was grateful he was with us. Especially when we heard, from the direction of the crowd, the long, agonized sound of a man crying out in the night.

AS WE NEARED THE SCHOOL and convent, we knew immediately that something was amiss. Torches were lit all up and down the walk in front, and in the back courtyard. Lights burned in the windows. People were gathering out front of the street, where two mules—the first white mules I'd ever seen in my life—were harnessed to a wagon. I even saw some of the boarding girls, in long wrappers, in the courtyard.

"Oh!" Elinora drew back into the shadows. "It's my uncle's wagon!"

"Are you sure?" I knew he wasn't expected until next week.

"Yes. Those are his mules, Contento and Angelica. He's had them for years. But he's a week early! Oh, what will we do? How will we get inside without being seen?"

"I think we can probably sneak inside, what with all the confusion."

Just then we heard a whisper through the iron gate. "Girls, girls. *Psst.*"

It was Gregorio. And Ramona. We crept toward them.

"You must come inside. They think you lost," Gregorio said. "Come, please. My wife, she get in trouble."

We started in the gate, then Elinora stopped and turned. "Not you," she said to the beggar. "You can't come in. Not now."

"Yes!" I pushed in front of her. "Gregorio, please. This

man is hungry and cold. And he is a carpenter. Please, can't we give him a place tonight?"

Gregorio would have given a place to Jesse James to get us in off the street. "Go to the back of barn," he told the beggar. "To the gate. I let you in."

The man nodded and left, and in the next instant, Elinora and I were pulled in through the gate and it clanged shut.

"Look, look," one girl yelled. It was Consuello herself. "There they are! I told you they weren't lost. There they are, Your Eminence."

A man came striding across the courtyard toward us. He was dressed in a buckskin riding coat with fringed cuffs. It was open in front. Under it he wore a black vest, a cravat, and a stiff collar as a priest wears. On his head was a wide-brimmed hat; on his feet, dusty boots. I don't know what a bishop is supposed to look like, but this one was handsome in a dignified, stern way. I saw by the way he nodded to people he brushed by that he was mannerly and concerned. That he was wellborn, distinguished, and certainly a man to be reckoned with.

"Elinora! Is it you? Is this my dear niece's child, then?" He held out his arms. Elinora ran to him. "Uncle, dear uncle." She burst into tears and threw herself down to kneel at his feet. "Oh, Uncle, forgive me. I have been naughty. But Lizzy wanted to sneak out this evening, and I couldn't let her go alone. I feared for her safety. I only went as a friend."

I stood like a mule bitten by a rattlesnake, taken aback by her lie and her acting. Around Elinora and Bishop Lamy gathered the nuns, the girls who boarded, the household help, and several strangers drawn off the street by the arrival of the Bishop.

Then two things happened. The Bishop drew Elinora to her feet and embraced her and everyone applauded. And Mother Magdalena stepped forward to grab me by the arm. "So, it was your doing! I might have guessed! Do you know what you put us through this night? You come along with me, young lady, right now!"

As she dragged me inside I saw Sister Roberta in the crowd. I met her eyes. They were kind and she was shaking her head as if to say, "No, no, you have the wrong culprit, Mother."

But she was the only one who knew it besides Ramona and Gregorio. And they were lucky Elinora didn't lay blame at their feet.

I got a switching that night from Mother Magdalena. The switch that she kept in her office bit through the long purple uniform and my underclothes. I had never been switched in my life, and the pain was nothing compared with the humiliation. Then I was made to sleep in what the girls called the dungeon. It was not a dungeon but a small room off the kitchen, with a hardboard bed with no mattress, no pillow, and a thin blanket. There was a high small window, a crucifix on the wall, and a nightstand with a bowl and a pitcher of cold water. One single candle glowed in a wall alcove below the crucifix.

The nuns called it the penance chamber.

I shivered and wept on the hardboard bed. When the house had quieted down, there came a single knock on the door, then it opened. I sat up, frightened.

"It's only me, child." It was Sister Roberta. She had brought a blanket, a pillow, and a warm brick wrapped in a towel. "I know how cold this cell can get at night. We Sisters sometimes use it when we are fasting and doing penance. You have no need to do penance, so I'm breaking all the rules.

Here." She put the pillow and blanket on the bed, and the heated brick at my feet. "Now wait."

She disappeared into the kitchen. In a few minutes she returned with a mug of hot chocolate.

"Thank you, Sister." I was shivering. She sat down on the bed and held me for a moment, clasping me to her ample bosom. "It wasn't your fault, now, was it?"

I shook my head no. "But the Bishop will hate me. Maybe he'll put me out."

"Don't you worry about Bishop Lamy. He isn't anybody's puppet. He likely knows already that his niece was lying."

"How?"

"That's why he's a bishop. If he speaks to you of it, you must tell him the truth."

"Why would he speak to me?"

"Because he speaks to all the students."

"But I'm a heretic. That's what Mother Magdalena called me tonight."

"If it's a heretic you are, then you're a beloved little heretic. The Bishop speaks to heretics, don't worry. Also," she lowered her voice, "he knows what a coquette his niece was. She got her own way in everything when she was here. And Elinora is just like her."

"You remember Elinora's mother?"

"Of course I do! She ran away and married when she was sixteen! Did Mother hit you hard?"

"Not too hard."

"Good. That means her heart wasn't in it. She herself wasn't sure you were guilty."

I would have hated to think what I'd feel like if her heart *was* in it.

"Here, I've brought some salve for your hurts. Put it on immediately. It will help. Go to sleep now. We'll talk another time. I'll be by early in the morning to get the pillow, blanket, and brick." She stood up. "Who is the man you brought back with you?"

"A beggar. He's traveling. He needs food and work. He's a carpenter, Sister. I thought he might help with the staircase. But now, after Mother Magdalena is so angry with me, she likely won't listen about him."

She was nodding slowly, yes, yes. And in the flickering light of the single candle, I made out a look in her eyes as if she knew more than I was saying. "She'll listen," she promised. "Now go to sleep. It's late."

THE CLATTERING OF KITCHEN utensils and the smell of bacon cooking woke me before first light. I lay shivering, not knowing where to hurt first. The heavy blanket, pillow, warming brick, and cocoa cup were gone. Who had taken them? And then I remembered. Sister Roberta. And a good thing she'd taken them, too. In the next instant, the door opened and Mother Magdalena stood there, her frame blocking all light and warmth from the kitchen. Over her arm she had some clothing. I recognized the calico dress Mrs. French had made for me.

She was going to send me away this day, I told myself. She was putting me out. Where would I go? I should have written to Uncle William already, yet here it was a week gone by and I hadn't. Likely I'd have to go up to the fort and live with Delvina. All those thoughts tumbled in my mind.

"Well? Up, lazy girl."

I sat up. My body screamed from stiffness and pain.

"I see you've slept in your uniform."

"I had nothing else. And it was so cold."

"Did you reflect on your sins?"

"Yes, ma'am."

"And did you reflect on what lying and disobedience bring you?"

I said yes, again. Humbly. It was what she wanted to hear. And I wondered if she knew that most of the girls told her what she wanted to hear, and not the truth. And I almost felt sorry for her.

"Well, on your feet, then. The Bishop wants to see you."

"Ma'am?" I was jolted awake.

"The Bishop. He will see you after mass. Put on these clothes so you don't look like the scalawag you are. Then have your breakfast here in the kitchen. Go use the necessary, wash, comb your hair, and make yourself presentable, now."

Then she was gone. The Bishop! So the Bishop himself was going to dismiss me, drum me out of the academy, as Uncle William said they did to derelicts in the army. My thoughts scrambled ahead of me in the cold room, like mice running from an owl. I tripped on things, shivered, hurt from the switching and sleeping on a board, and my teeth chattered when I tried to wash, because the water in the basin had a thin sheeting of ice. I didn't wash. I combed my hair. It was flyaway and curly and brown. How I envied girls with smooth bouncing curls! I ran outside to the necessary, ran back in again, and begged Ramona for warm water, to wash properly in the kitchen. She gave me some frijoles, eggs, and bacon for breakfast, which I ate hastily because I wanted to run out to the barn, not only to feed Ben but to see if the beggar man was all right.

Quickly I crossed the back courtyard in the cold. The barn

was warm, and the familiar smell of hay and horses and manure comforted me. I fed Ben, promising him I would take
him out later when we went with Mrs. Lacey. Not knowing if
there would be a later. Or if it would be sooner, when the
Bishop dismissed me.

"He's a beautiful horse," someone said.

I turned around. It was the beggar man. He was feeding
the Bishop's white mules.

"You know about horses?"

"I know they are one of God's finer creatures."

"Did they feed you and take care of you and your mule?"

"I have been provided for, thank you."

"Well, I have to go now. I have to see the Bishop."

He smiled, and I blushed. It sounded so pompous. "I
mean, I think he's angry about Elinora's and my being out last
night, and wants to scold. But if I get a chance, I'm going to
tell him there's a carpenter in the barn looking for work. I
promise."

He nodded knowingly. And went back to caring for the
white mules.

THE HALLS OF THE SCHOOL were full of people who had
just come out of the chapel after hearing the Bishop's mass. I
had to push my way through. I found the Bishop in his study,
at his desk. It was the kind my mama had called a secretary.
On it were two silver candlesticks. The ceiling was heavy cedar
beams; Indian blankets were on the floor. A fire burned in the
hearth, and there were wooden chests, decorated with leather,
under both windows. The Bishop wore a black robe, with a
red sash around his middle.

"Ah, our little heretic." He smiled and got up.

I did not know what to do. If I'd been wearing boots I'd be shivering in them. I knew that. Was I supposed to throw myself at his feet, as Elinora had done? Call him "Eminence"?

I was darned if I'd throw myself at anybody's feet. Uncle William would never forgive me.

And then I saw it. The cat. Pure white it was, on a cushion in the corner by the hearth, nursing four white kittens.

I forgot all about the Bishop. "Oh," I said. And I ran to kneel by the cat. I stroked its soft head, and it purred and licked my hand. "Oh, what adorable kittens."

The Bishop coughed. It was a dry sound, and I remembered how Sister Roberta had said he always returned from his trips with a cough. And we hadn't yet fetched bark from the wild chokecherry tree for his cough syrup. I must remind Sister Roberta.

Or was the cough intentional, for me, because I hadn't greeted him properly? Embarrassed, I stood up. "I'm sorry, sir. I had to leave my cats back in Independence."

I curtsied.

One hand rubbing his chin, he nodded, pleased. "You like cats, then?"

"Oh, I love them. But Daddy wouldn't let me bring one on the Trail."

He gestured to a chair and told me to sit. I did so. He took a chair a bit away from me. "Isabella is a good mouser," he said.

"Isabella?"

"Yes, I named her after Queen Isabella of Spain. The kittens were born while I was away."

I looked at them longingly. "What will you do with them all?"

"They will go in the barn, after Isabella has taught them to be mousers. Well, what do you think of Santa Fe?"

We were making pleasant conversation, yet somehow I felt something more was going on here. I felt that he was taking my measure. Very well, then, I would show him I was no phony-pony like all the other girls around here. I would show him I had mettle. If he was going to dismiss me, there would be no changing his mind, anyway.

"I tend to think what Zebulon Pike thought, sir. The adobe houses look like flat-bottomed boats on the Ohio River."

He laughed. It had a boyish sound. "I tend to think so, too. For years after I came here I missed Paris." Then he coughed again, and I knew it was a true cough. "Excuse me." He took a sip of water from a nearby glass. His finely knit brows came together. "I hear you lost your mother on the way to Santa Fe."

"She took the fever. We buried her in the desert. She was too young to die."

"*Achaque quiere la muerte para lleverse a los mortales,*" he said.

"I don't speak Spanish."

" 'Death needs no pretext to carry off the living.' I have seen much of it, child. I am sure your beloved mother is with God, looking down on you this minute."

A hush seemed to come over the room. Of a sudden the chatter and the bustle from the hall was gone. I saw the goodness in this man. I felt it like a warmth between us. And a sense of peace came over me.

"I hope she is looking down," I said. "I hope she tells God to not let you put me out of the academy."

He cocked his head. His dignified, gentle hands made a peak on his crossed knee. "You think I am going to put you out?"

"After last night, yes sir."

"But last night was not your fault. Do you think I do not know that?"

"How?" I asked. "Elinora told you—"

He held up a hand to silence me. "People tell me all kinds of things, child. Sister Roberta came and cautioned me. It seems my niece lied."

I held my breath. The way the words tripped off his tongue left no room for surprise. Or anger. He smiled sadly this time. "She wants to make a good impression on me. She needed a scapegoat. I will have a talk with her about her ways."

A talk? Anger flooded my veins. "I was punished," I said.

"I know, dear child. For which I do apologize. Believe me, when I have a talk with Elinora it will affect her worse than Mother Magdalena's punishment affected you."

He looked at me levelly as he said this. And I believed him. And almost felt sorry for Elinora.

"I hope the blanket and pillow and warming brick kept you from being too cold in the penance room last night."

I gasped. "You know about that?"

"Sister Roberta does not go against Mother Magdalena's wishes as blatantly as I fear she might. I suggested she provide things to make the night bearable for you. Was it?"

"Yes sir, thank you."

"As for the punishment you received at the hands of Mother Magdalena, you must understand. She is responsible for the safety of all these girls. She sometimes gets overzealous. I do not believe in corporal punishment. But she cannot allow running on the streets at night. Mayhem occurs. Last night when you and my niece were running about out there, a prisoner was dragged from his cell in the jail and hanged by a mob."

I drew in my breath. "They hanged Billy the Kid?"

He coughed once more and gave me a narrow, questioning gaze. "They hanged the one prisoner in the jail. I did not hear he was Billy the Kid."

"Oh, sir, forgive me. Mrs. Lacey calls him that."

"Ah, yes. Mrs. Lacey has a fanciful imagination."

"But why did they hang him? It's so terrible!"

"Yes, it is, child. But terrible things happen on Santa Fe's streets every night. That is why Mother Magdalena punished you so severely. She believed you to be at fault. Let me say that the good are often punished unfairly. However, I mind that you do not wish to hear any homilies now. So please, allow me to make amends."

"Amends?"

"Yes. Tell me some way I can make your life more bearable here. I know you miss your father and your home, and mourn your mother. Is there something I can do to keep you from thinking we still cherish the methods of the Inquisition?"

The Inquisition? What is that? I must look it up.

He was watching me, studying me closely with blue eyes that had a fire and a tenderness in them, all at the same time. "A favor I might grant?" he pushed.

I nodded. "Two. But not for me."

He laughed again. "A true American. And not such an infidel after all. Ask."

"There is a man in the barn. A beggar. I brought him home with us last night, even though Elinora—well, never mind that. Gregorio put him in the barn. He has no work, and he is a carpenter. I thought that since you need a staircase built in the chapel you might give him work."

"Ah, the staircase." He sighed and leaned back in his chair. "Such a dilemma. The nuns have been conducting a novena to Saint Joseph, and I have been praying on the matter myself. They look to me to perform miracles, which, of course, I can't. But perhaps you, with your outsider's opinions of us, have the best solution for the moment. Have the hungry carpenter take a look at it. Hunger has pushed some men to greatness. It provides a special vision. Yes, I can do that. What else?"

"Ramona is in desperate need of a new cast-iron stove in the kitchen. The one she has smokes. And burns her cakes and pies."

"A new stove for Ramona," he said.

"Yes, sir, if it isn't too much to ask."

He nodded, seeing more in my face than I willingly let him see. He stood up and held out his hand. "Come, child, kneel so I can bless you."

Well, I supposed kneeling now wouldn't be throwing myself at his feet. I did so. Oh, it felt strange, kneeling before a Catholic bishop. But then he put his hand on my head, and his touch was gentle, like the warmth of the sun. And he prayed in Latin over me.

How can you be angry or contentious when somebody prays over you? You can truly be an infidel and it will make your mind humble even while your spirit soars.

When he was finished, I stood and curtsied again and started to flee the room.

"Wait."

I stopped. "Yes sir?"

"Would you like a kitten?"

My eyes went wide. "For my very own?"

"Ownership of one of God's creatures is a responsibility. You must always care for it. And respect it."

"Oh, sir, I would love a kitten!" Then I scowled. "Respect it?"

"You must always respect yourself. Your fellow humans, the beasts God made. All are worthy of respect. Even the juniper tree."

I nodded, touched. *This is a great man,* I decided. I wished he were my uncle. No offense, of course, to Uncle William. "I will respect it always," I said.

"Very well. Sister Roberta cares for my office. She has the key. I shall tell her to allow you in here, when I am not busy, to visit and to pick one out. Also, you may tell your beggar-man friend that I wish to see him. Now."

I could not believe my good fortune. I curtsied again. "Thank you, oh, thank you!" And then I fled.

I heard him coughing, as I ran down the hall.

10

OUT IN THE HALLWAY the first one I ran into was Mother Magdalena.

"And where are you off to in such a hurry? Class?"

"No, ma'am. I'm on an errand for the Bishop."

"I see. I assume that after this important errand you will appear in class? Properly dressed?"

"But my uniform is all wrinkled."

"Ramona has pressed it for you. I expect you to get back immediately to your routine, which includes taking Mrs. Lacey to the cemetery this afternoon. She has been asking after you."

Inwardly I groaned. I had forgotten to visit Mrs. Lacey with her breakfast. I hoped Ramona had remembered.

Mother Magdalena dismissed me with a curt nod. I thought it oafish of her not to apologize for switching me when I had been declared innocent. But I was too excited about the beggar man to care. Or to worry anymore about my aches and pains.

He was in the barn, sweeping. "Oh sir." I ran up to him. "Sir."

"I am not accustomed to be so hailed." He stopped sweeping. "Yes. You have seen the Bishop?"

"Yes. And he wants to speak with you right now! About the staircase!"

"I owe you many thanks. Where do I find this bishop?"

"In the house, in his study. I can take you to him."

He brushed himself off, rearranged his shawl, and ran a hand through his long graying hair. "I am not presentable."

"Oh, he doesn't mind. Come. I have to go to class."

"Wait. Let me get my tools."

I don't know what I expected when he spoke of tools. But it was a small sack. "That holds your tools?" I asked.

"A saw, a T square, and a hammer." He looked at me with those old brown eyes of his. "What else is needed?"

I nodded and we walked together across the courtyard. "Where do you come from?" I asked.

He raised an arm and pointed in the direction of the Santa Fe Trail. "Out there," he said, "in the land of vast spaces and long silences. Where the red bluffs are. And the flowering cactus. Where the desert changes colors."

I nodded. "I came on the Santa Fe Trail, too."

I took him in through the kitchen. Ramona looked up from her work, smiled at him, and said, *"Me alegro de verte bien"* to him. He nodded and smiled.

"You understand Spanish," I said. "What did she say?"

" 'I am glad to see you in good health.' "

"Does she know you?"

"No, but it was a fine welcome."

The door of the Bishop's study was open, but he was again at the desk, writing. I knocked on the doorjamb. He looked up, smiled, and came toward us.

"Bishop Lamy, this is the carpenter," I said.

Then, horrified, I turned to the beggar man, realizing that I did not even know his name. How should I introduce him?

"Thank you, Lizzy, you may go," the Bishop said. I left. I walked slowly, and before I knew it the Bishop and the carpenter were coming up behind me on their way to the chapel at the end of the hall. They were deep in conversation as they walked by me, unaware I was even there. But I heard some bits of what was said.

"No room was left for the staircase to the choir loft," Bishop Lamy was explaining. "The only alternative left for a builder now is to tear down the choir loft and rebuild it. But that would be a great expense. The other choice is a ladder. But how can I have these little girls climbing a ladder? You see my problem?"

There were some words I did not hear. I halted in front of the door to French class. At the end of the hall, the Bishop had opened the door to the chapel, and they stood just inside. The Bishop was pointing to the back of the chapel, and then together they walked out of my sight.

Quietly I crept down the hall to the chapel door and peeked in. They were at the end, in the space where a staircase should be. They were in a world of their own, talking. Then I saw the beggar man step into the space, reach out his old hands, and make motions as if he were measuring. He stepped around in a circle, his hands extended, his eyes looking upward. Measuring. All the while his lips were moving silently.

"Yes," he said to the Bishop, finally. "I can build your staircase. But it must be a spiral one."

"Spiral!" The Bishop's voice was filled with pleasant surprise. "I never thought of that! And the nuns had several car-

penters in to consult with. No one mentioned doing it spiral.
But can you do it?"

"I can."

"Fine. I will open an account for you at the lumberyard in
town. You have only to go and order what you need. Give me
an estimate of cost this afternoon. Can you do that?"

"With all due respect," the man answered, "I would prefer
not to do so until tomorrow."

"Oh?" the Bishop said.

"I know tonight is the last night of the novena the nuns are
making to Saint Joseph. And out of respect for that, I would
start when it is finished."

"You know about the novena?"

"The little girl told me."

"Ah, yes. Of course, you are right. We must wait out of respect to Saint Joseph."

I started back down the hall to change my dress as Mother
Magdalena had instructed me to do. Had I told the beggar
man about the novena? I could not remember.

AFTER FRENCH CLASS I approached Sister Roberta. "The
Bishop is coughing," I said.

She was stuffing some books into a leather case. "One
week here and already you're giving me intelligence about the
Bishop's health." But her eyes were twinkling. Then they got
sad. "Thank you, Lizzy. I've been so busy. But then, he had no
business coming back a week early from his trip, did he?"

"I have to get permission to go with you," I said.

"I have free time this afternoon."

"Mother Magdalena is still angry with me. She'll never
allow it."

"Well, I do have some say around here. If I get you off from classes, will you come?"

"Can you do that?"

"I have uncommon powers," she said as she went out to the hallway.

I stared at her broad back. *She's heard about our trip to the witch's house,* I told myself. *I wonder who else knows? Probably everybody.*

But she must have had uncommon powers, because that afternoon, we set out for the nearest branch of the river. Sister Roberta had packed some delicacies in a basket. I rode Ben, and she rode a horse from the stables—sidesaddle, until we got away from town. Then she hitched up her skirts and rode astride.

The warm November sun felt good on my face and my aching body, even through the purple school uniform. That afternoon, Sister Roberta showed me how to recognize the herbs she needed and how to take the bark from the wild choke-cherry tree.

While we worked, we talked. "I heard about the hanging of the prisoner last night. Terrible," she said.

I told her I had met him, and I told her how.

"Mrs. Lacey is a curious person. But a good friend to have," she told me. "Tell me, why don't you, about the witch's house? Is it as everyone says inside?"

"How did you know?" I asked. I felt myself blushing for my foolishness.

"By now everyone knows. Not much can be kept secret in that school. Well? Does she really have an owl named Sitting Bull?"

I told her about Dolores's house. "You don't hold with magic, then?" I asked.

"Magic is all around us," she said, gesturing to the river, to the herbs, to the birds overhead. "Believing keeps us alive. Did you hear yet about the magic of the bell in San Miguel Chapel over on De Vargas Street?"

"No, but I saw the chapel."

"Mrs. Lacey hasn't taken you there yet? The church was built in 1610. The bell came from Spain. The story is that an old blind man would go to the chapel at noon every day and pray to Saint Cecelia, who is the patron saint of musicians. Whenever he prayed, the bell would ring. On its own. And for as long as it rang, he could see."

I stared at her. She went on, casually picking herbs.

"They knew he could see because he could tell them what the church looked like. He could name the colors in the paintings, talk about the carved work around the altar. But as soon as the bell stopped, his blindness returned. The priests tried ringing the bell themselves, but it did no good. He was blind when they rang it. Only a few years ago did the bell fall from the tower in a storm. Now it sits on a wooden frame on the floor. The blind man died, and it has never rung by itself again."

I shivered in the warm sunlight.

"Now that's believing," she said. "If you want to call it magic, then do."

I told her more about the witch's house. The conversation was pleasant in the quiet of the riverbank. I knew I could trust her. I told her about my cats back home and how the Bishop had said I could have a kitten. I told her my fears that I would never hear from my father. It was almost as good as having my friend Cassie at my side.

"OH, THE STAIRCASE!" Mrs. Lacey stopped midway in our climb up the hill to the cemetery later that afternoon and clasped her hands over her slight bosom. "I can't believe we finally have a carpenter to build it! And all thanks to you, Lizzy. You were sent here for a reason, child! God bless you." Her eyes glistened with tears. "Now my Robert will rest in peace."

"But why wouldn't he until now?" I made bold to ask.

We recommenced our climb. "Because of my sins," she said.

"God doesn't punish one person for another's sins," I told her. "Even we Methodists know that."

"In this case, I'm afraid He will, Lizzy. Because Robert's sin was caused by me. I'll tell you about it sometime. Meanwhile I have a more immediate worry. And since you are my friend, I will share it with you. And then you must share one with me."

I trudged wearily up the hill, leading Ben, who was lugging the heavy blankets Sister Roberta had sent for Delvina. I was pure spent from my expedition with Sister Roberta earlier, but I couldn't neglect Mrs. Lacey any more. The welts from the switching were starting to hurt again, despite the salve Sister Roberta had given me to put on them. And my limbs still hurt from sleeping on the board bed. Too, it had been a long trip through town this day, what with Mrs. Lacey shaking her fists at certain people and stopping to scold them for hanging her friend Billy the Kid. She was all mooded up over it and cast down at the same time.

"Suppose I don't have a worry to give you in return?" I asked.

"You do. You have many. And that's the way it works. Friends share worries. And good news. Do you have any good news?"

"Only that the carpenter told the Bishop the staircase will be spiral."

"Spiral—how brilliant! Now, why didn't any of the other carpenters the Bishop spoke with come up with that idea? I tell you, this man was sent to us by God, Lizzy."

"Tell me your worry," I said.

She sighed. "I'm failing, Lizzy. I know it. My mind is going and I have many ailments. Every day I feel weaker and weaker. Sometimes I can scarce fetch the strength to come here to the cemetery."

"I could come for you," I offered.

"Dear girl, that is not my worry. It is that if my mind goes altogether, the nuns will baptize me Catholic before I die."

"But you're Methodist. They know that."

"Yes, but I left my home in Richmond in such a hurry, I have no proof that I was baptized anything. And they always require proof, these Catholics. Everything about you must be printed on a piece of paper, for them to accept it. Promise me." She reached out her hand and gripped my arm. "Promise me you will not let them baptize me Catholic. If I am to meet my Maker, I would do so Methodist. It's a good religion. It's held me in good stead all my life."

I looked at her with doubt in my eyes, I am ashamed to say. "How can I stop them?" I asked.

"You can't. But if you find out that they've done it, you can have it voided."

"Void a baptism?"

"Yes."

"How?"

"Simple. A bag of asafetida around the neck will do it. What the nuns use for croup."

I blinked at her, unbelieving. "Asafetida?"

"Yes. It voids the baptism. Don't look at me like that. I know from what I speak. I have it from the highest sources here in Santa Fe. Where they know about things like spells and wishes, sin and forgiveness, and the art of magic."

"Who?" I demanded. "Who told you this?"

She stopped climbing again to look at me full face. "Do you think you are the first to visit Dolores la Penca? Do you think you discovered her?"

"Oh, Mrs. Lacey, I'm so ashamed of that visit. Everybody knows about it and is belaboring the matter."

"They're jealous. And curious. They all would like to visit her. Even the nuns, believe me."

I remembered then Sister Roberta's interest and questions. "Did Dolores tell you that's the way to void a baptism, then?"

"She did. And though others may scoff at her, or pretend to scoff, she holds sway over everyone with her opinions, believe me. People dare not disbelieve her."

"All right, Mrs. Lacey," I said. "I will do whatever you wish if they baptize you."

"Good. Now, tell me what your worry is," she pushed. "I know something is troubling you."

A lot of matters troubled me. But I gave my attention to the one at hand. "Sister Roberta wants me to keep her apprised of Delvina's condition. She wants to bring her into the convent just before the baby comes."

"Well! I wondered when those Polly Pureheart nuns would get around to putting their attention to a real problem. Come, we will ask Delvina. Today."

"You mean I can meet her?" I stood dumbfounded.

"Well, do you know a way to ask her without meeting her? Perhaps you do," she said, leading me across the mesa. "Perhaps you learned something from that witch after all."

11

❖

WE BOTH HEARD THE sound of a baby crying, at the same time.

We stopped and stared at each other. Then Mrs. Lacey said, "Hurry." And she betook herself across the flat dry ground toward the only remaining building as if she were fourteen again. It was an old two-story, crumbling building. I followed her.

Inside, on the first floor, she led me to a small room that had holes in the walls that gave a magnificent view but also let in the cold.

On the floor, huddled in old dusty blankets, was a young woman. The baby was wailing out its misery, for it was that time of day when the cold started to descend.

"Oh, Mrs. Lacey," she said, reaching out her hand. "Oh, you have come. *Madre de Dios,* I thought you would never come."

Never had I seen such a beautiful woman in my life. Her face had the sweet roundness of perfection to it. Her eyes were so blue they would make the sky jealous. Her hair was richly dark and fell about her shoulders where it had become unpinned.

In her arms she held a tiny likeness of herself. A newborn baby. It had stopped crying now and was mewing like a cat.

"Delvina, Delvina, child. How did you have this baby by yourself? And when?"

"Last night," she said in a gentle voice tinged with tiredness. "But I was not alone. Lozen was here. She helped me."

"Lozen! Oh, I wish I had seen her. How good of her. And when did she leave?"

"She stayed the night with me. She fetched water, made a fire. See? There are the remains." She pointed, and sure enough, the charred remains of a wood fire sat nearby.

Then she noticed me. "Ah, this is the *muchachita bonita* who comes with you every day to visit Robert's grave, is she not?"

"Yes, this is Lizzy Enders."

"Hello, Lizzy, how are you?"

"How are *you*?" I asked. "You need help. Sister Roberta at the school wanted me to ask you when you expected your lying-in."

"Tell Sister Roberta it came sooner than expected."

"I've brought blankets. Here." I spread them over her. "But you and the baby need to get into someplace proper and warm. Sister Roberta wants you to come to the convent. She said they have a place for you."

"Oh, I don't know. It wouldn't be safe."

"It's safer than here."

"For everyone in the convent, I mean. If my husband finds out I'm there, there's no telling what evil he'll try to do."

"The Bishop is back," I told her. I thought of the Bishop's strong, distinguished face, of his no-nonsense manner. "He won't let any harm come to anyone. You must come today!" I appealed to Mrs. Lacey. "Please!"

"Lizzy is right. And she is going to get on her horse right now and ride back and have a wagon brought for you and the child. Aren't you, Lizzy?"

I got up. "Yes."

Delvina lay back on the blankets. "I'm afraid I'm not as strong as I thought," she said. "I don't feel well. So all I can hope is that the nuns will find a place for my baby."

I was already running across the ground toward Ben. "I'll be back very soon," I yelled over my shoulder.

BLACK SHADOWS ALREADY LAY in the lee of adobe walls as I rode Ben back through town. It was against the law to race your mount in the street. I had been told that by Mother Magdalena. Weariness sat on my shoulders and on top of my head as I walked Ben as fast as I could. I thought about the other law Sister Roberta had told me about the day she told me to keep her apprised of Delvina's condition.

"Midwives must be licensed in Santa Fe. And that license must be granted by a municipal judge. Also, they must have a certificate from their parish priest that says they know how to administer baptism. That's why we must get her back here. She must have a proper midwife."

I giggled, wondering if Lozen would be considered licensed.

Then I frowned, worrying about the baby. I hadn't even asked if it was a boy or girl. And suppose it died before we got it back to the convent? It would end up in Limbo. And I would be blamed. I should have brought it along with me and not left it in the cold. But then I wouldn't be able to manage Ben so well.

Maybe I or Mrs. Lacey should have baptized the baby. Was it possible for a heretic to do so? Oh, I was so tired and confused! I'd been on the run since early this morning, I'd scarce slept last night, and my head buzzed with weariness. I rode past the plaza. The last of the merchants were packing up their wares. Some Indians from nearby pueblos, who also came to sell, had wrapped themselves in blankets to guard the meat they would leave hanging overnight in the cold. It hung on ropes suspended from the portal of the Governor's Palace. I knew those shapes were venison, turkey, and even bear. But they took on a dark, menacing appearance.

I passed the U.S. Army quartermaster's depot, two blocks from the convent. "We're almost there, Ben," I said.

When I got inside the gates of the school, the first person I saw was Gregorio. I was so glad to see him that I slipped off Ben, nearly fell, and he came to help me up.

"*Muchachita,* what has happened? Where is Mrs. Lacey?"

I was unsteady on my feet and held on to Ben as I blurted out my story. Then I collapsed.

Gregorio carried me inside. I protested, but he would not listen. In through the kitchen, where he shouted for his wife. "Bring her to the nuns. Get Bishop Lamy from his supper!"

In the next minute the whole place became alive with mayhem. Ramona sat me at the table and sent a servant for Mother Magdalena and the Bishop. Both came into the kitchen and I told my story again. Bishop Lamy didn't shilly-shally. He ordered Gregorio to get out the wagon and go and fetch home Mrs. Lacey, the baby, and Delvina. Sister Roberta was to go with him. She ran for some remedies.

"I want to go, too, please," I begged. "They won't know where to find them."

"They know where the fort is," Bishop Lamy spoke kindly

but firmly. "And the deserted building. That woman Delvina should have been brought here sooner." He turned to Mother Magdalena.

"You know who her husband is, Your Eminence," she said. "I couldn't endanger my girls."

"This is my church," he said. "And my school and convent. It is a safe house. A place of asylum." Then he stopped himself. If he was going to have a difference of opinion with Mother Magdalena, he would save it until later. He looked at me. "This child is exhausted," he said.

"She went with Sister Roberta this afternoon to pick herbs." It was Elinora. All the girls who boarded were in the kitchen now, too. It was supper hour, and they'd come in from the student dining room to see what the fuss was about.

"I told you, Elinora," the Bishop said, "that you were to keep silent the rest of this day, did I not?"

Elinora flushed, sniffed, and went back to the dining room. Apparently she and her uncle had had their little "talk." She did not look at all happy.

"Who delivered the baby?" the Bishop then asked me.

I had hoped nobody would ask. But he was smart, this bishop. I looked up at him mutely, hoping he would not insist. He saw something in my face, I suppose.

"Tell me, child."

I knew everyone was staring at me, but felt only the eyes of the Bishop, pulling the truth out of me like a bad tooth. "She said Lozen," I told him.

He showed no surprise. He did not ask who Lozen was. Others did. "Who? Who?" The question went around the room until the Bishop held up his hand to silence everyone.

"Feed this child," he then told Ramona. "Some of that

good *sopa de vermicile,* then see that she has a hot bath and is put to bed in the guest room. Make sure she is all right. Call me if she isn't."

He nodded and smiled at me encouragingly. And I knew then that he knew about Lozen. I did not have to explain. He turned and left the room.

Everyone went back to their business. I ate the *sopa de vermicile,* which was vermicelli soup and very delicious. I was about starved. Then Ramona took me upstairs to the guest room. I'd never seen it before. It had a highpost bed. One of Gregorio's assistants soon had a roaring fire in the hearth. Another servant filled a copper tub with hot water. I took a hot bath while Ramona went to fetch my nightgown and my clothes for the morning. I took the bath without my chemise and pantalets on and enjoyed the sensuous sudsy hot water into which Ramona had put some lavender. She came back and washed my hair, pouring more hot water over it. Then, while I sat in front of the fire in my nightdress, she dried my hair with a towel and brushed it until I was drowsy. Then she pulled back the quilt on the feather bed, left a lighted candle, and said she would be back.

I lay in the feather bed, feeling as if I were in Mama's arms, watching the flickering shadows from the candlelight on the whitewashed walls. In a wall crevice was the Virgin, the snake under her feet. I was so weary her face looked like Mama's. I tried to stay awake, to listen for the sound of the wagon outside when they came back with Mrs. Lacey and Delvina and the baby. But I was a weak-spined sissy-boots. And I fell asleep.

12

✦

WHEN I AWOKE the next morning, it was to the smell of coffee as I lay in a feather bed in a room with a crackling fire and no Elinora to badger me. I thought I was in heaven.

There stood one of Ramona's helpers, a girl they called Carlotta, with a tray of food. I sat up, embarrassed. "Oh, I must get up," I said.

"You stay in bed." Firmly she put the tray down in front of me, then smiled. "Mother Magdalena say so."

"Mother Magdalena?"

"*Si*." She drew open the curtains to let in the sun.

"But it's late. I must go to class."

"Is Saturday," she told me.

Saturday. I decided that I would eat the delicious breakfast, then go to see Mrs. Lacey. I set myself to the task. Breakfast in bed! Never in my life had I had such a luxury! And sent by Mother Magdalena!

Bishop Lamy and she must have talked, and this was by way of making up for her treatment of me. Either that or she was simply following Bishop Lamy's orders. No matter. The breakfast was delicious. I languished in the treatment and my mood lifted. This day I would finally write to my uncle William. And Cassie. Dear Cassie! Over a week here, and I hadn't written yet. She must think me dead.

Then I heard some hammering in the distance, from the other side of the wall, where the chapel must be. *Oh!* I jumped out of bed. *The beggar man must be working! I must go see!* But first I had to wash, dress, visit Mrs. Lacey, and feed Ben. I had so much to do!

As I slipped my dress over my head, I remembered that last night was the final night of the novena to Saint Joseph. And I hadn't attended the services.

I went downstairs. The place was quiet except for the sound of hammering from the chapel. The first people I ran into were Elinora and the other boarding girls.

They were talking in the hallway, voices low. They were gathered around Elinora in a very protective way. Something was wrong.

"Well, I hope you're happy," Rosalyn said.

"About what?"

"You got to sleep in the best guest room," said Consuello.

"And you've got that old carpenter in there hammering away. That old beggar man. How is Saint Joseph supposed to do his miracle for us now, with that stinking old man in there making a mess?" Consuello asked.

"The Bishop hired him," I said.

"Don't you understand?" Consuello put her face close to mine. "We're all waiting to see what Saint Joseph will do. How can he do anything now when he thinks we have the problem solved?"

"I'm sure Saint Joseph knows better," I told her.

She threw her hands up in dismay. "That's how much you know! Saint Joseph will think we have no faith in him!"

"Because we let a beggar man have work?" I asked.

"Would you help a bunch of people who have a novena to ask for your help, who then go and say, 'Never mind. We've found somebody, we don't need you'?" Now it was Winona who put the question to me.

"We're on our way to the Bishop's farm. We told him before he left this morning that we had important matters to discuss," Lucy put in. "We are invited to lunch. At lunch we will ask him to stop that man from his building."

I gasped. "But you can't do that!"

"I'd like to know why not," Lucy said. "Elinora's uncle will see the reasoning of our argument. He is most devoted to Saint Joseph himself. That beggar man will be out of here by tonight. You'll see."

Something was amiss. Why was Elinora not flinging accusations at me? Why was she standing there, eyes downcast? Why did Winona have a protective arm around her shoulder?

"What's wrong with Elinora?" I asked.

Consuello sighed wearily. "Of course, you wouldn't know. Since you were so busy being pampered last night." She brushed some hair away from Elinora's face with all the tenderness of a mother. "Elinora has a calling."

I just stared.

"You see how much you don't understand?" Consuello snapped.

"No, no," Elinora said in a gentle, begging tone. "She isn't of the Faith. How could she?"

"A calling. To become a nun," Consuello spoke the words carefully, as if to a child. "She wants to take vows."

"And marry Jesus," Lucy added. "Isn't it thrilling?"

"Don't you understand?" Winona asked.

I studied Elinora through narrowed eyes. I thought she had a deceptive cast to her. I understood, all right. I understood that her "calling" was a fancy bit of acting to put herself back in her uncle's good graces. And that she would use it to get rid of the beggar-man carpenter so they could sit around sucking their thumbs and waiting for their miracle.

I understood that if the Bishop believed her about having a calling, he might let the carpenter go. But I composed myself. "Well, have a nice lunch," I said.

Consuello turned, a sly smile on her face. "You had your night of pampering in the best guest room. That's only because the Bishop thought you were sick. He can't have sickness here. But don't think for one minute that you're his pet."

"I'm not anybody's pet," I said. "I don't want to be. Neither do I want to sit around and wait for some stupid miracle when we have a perfectly good carpenter in there building the staircase right now."

"We're going to tell the Bishop your sentiments," Winona promised. "He'll hear what you said. And he'll hear what Elinora has to tell him about her calling. Come along, girls. Gregorio is waiting with the wagon."

I DECIDED NOT TO tell Mrs. Lacey that the carpenter might be dismissed. It would distress her so. Her room was on the bottom floor so she did not have to climb stairs. It was commodious and filled with her favorite pieces of furniture, rugs, candlesticks, and mementos. They had already brought her breakfast. Sunlight flooded the room, which looked out on the courtyard. She was in a chair, leaning her head against a pillow. I could smell the heated hops inside it.

"You've got your neuralgia back," I said.

"Oh, my dear, I've had a terrible night. The pain! It must have been the night air."

"Mrs. Lacey, I wanted to go back for you. They wouldn't let me."

"I should think not! They tell me you collapsed from exhaustion!"

"Yes, and I'm so ashamed! I never fainted in my life. I feel like such a sissy-boots. I tried to stay awake until you came back last night, but I couldn't even do that."

"You poor child, of course not. You had a terrible day. Tell me, have you any news?"

"Of what?"

"Delvina. They won't let me see her. And I probably couldn't get out of this chair, anyway. They say she is dying."

"She can't be!" Why I said such, I didn't know. Certainly women died all the time from having babies. But why hadn't the other girls told me? *Silly,* I thought. *They don't care if Delvina is dying. They care only about their stupid miracle.*

Mrs. Lacey took my hand in both of hers. "She lost a lot of blood. I'm so worried they'll blame Lozen. But she did her best. She wasn't supposed to deliver babies, you know. She had no license. But who else was there to help her? Only Jesse James, and what does he know?"

I blinked. "Jesse James?"

"Yes, of course. He kept watch. That's what Delvina told

me. Oh, I must tell him to be careful. I'll leave a note for him today. If the authorities go after Lozen, they'll be on his scent."

Was she beset with her fancies again? I looked at her. The eyes that gazed back were rheumy, red rimmed. She was sickly. The night air and the excitement of last evening had set her back.

"You must do some favors for me today, dear, will you?"

"Of course," I said abstractedly.

"First you must try to get into the sickroom and see Delvina. I hear the Bishop is coming from his farm tonight to baptize the baby."

"The baby! Is it well? And is it a boy or a girl?"

"A darling little baby girl. And well. The baptism will be a precaution. I wish you to bring Delvina this and let me know how she is doing." She held out a soft, warm shawl, so delicate in weave and color that it looked like an angel's wing.

"I'll do my best," I promised.

"And you must take this note and leave it under a stone on top of the cubicle that holds the lantern for my son." She handed me a piece of folded vellum.

"You're not going to the cemetery this afternoon?" I asked.

"I want to, child. But I'm considerably weakened from this neuralgia. So you must be my emissary. The note is for Jesse James. Let no one see it. It will warn him that the authorities may be about, and he must stay away from the fort."

I didn't, for a moment, believe that Jesse James was at the fort. Or even in New Mexico. But I promised to do it.

"Make sure my son's lantern is lit," she instructed. "Don't wait about for Jesse. He won't come out if you're there, much as you admire him. Just leave the note. I don't think you'll see

Lozen at all, of course. Now give me one of those powders Sister Roberta left for me and some water. There's a good girl. I don't know what I'd do without you, Lizzy."

I gave her the powder and water, covered her with an afghan, and straightened the hops-filled pillow. Then I kissed her forehead. "I'll be by to see you later," I said.

THE CHAPEL WAS DESERTED. There was a note tacked on the door by Mother Magdalena. "By order of the Mother Superior: The carpenter is working inside. If you wish to pray, slip in silently and stay in the front pews. Please do not approach him. He is very shy, and his work must proceed without interruption."

I slipped in silently. But I did not go into the front pews. I walked down the center aisle toward the back. The scene was strange. I don't know what I expected, but not this. All around where the staircase would be, he had already removed some church pews, leaving others behind the area still standing. There were candles, in all manner of holders, lit in profusion where he was working. They cast a wondrous glow. And there were tubs of water in which sat his wood.

"Hello," I said.

He turned and smiled. He had already sawed some wood, and sawdust was sprinkled on the floor. "Can I fetch you anything?" I asked.

"No, no, I have all I need, thank you."

"Are you still sleeping in the barn?"

He nodded. "I have a nice, cozy corner. And they feed me in great plenty."

"Oh, I'm so glad. But how can you do all this without a helper?"

"Oh, I've been a carpenter for years. We work best alone."

"Tools," I said. "They have tools here. I saw them in the shed. If you need any, I'm sure you have only to ask."

"Thank you, but my hammer, T square, and saw will suffice." He stopped working then and looked at me. I thought he appeared to be a bit younger this morning. "You are the only girl who has bothered to come and inquire of my needs. The others rush in here and out."

"Mother Magdalena has told people not to bother you. I'm disobeying her by talking to you," I admitted.

"The others stare and point at me. I hear their whispers. 'We prayed for Saint Joseph to send us a miracle, and look what we got. A broken-down old man. He couldn't make a staircase in a hundred years.'"

"I'm sorry," I said. "It's because they made a novena to Saint Joseph. Now it is over and they await a miracle. And they think Saint Joseph will be insulted if you do the work while they are waiting for him to respond."

He looked at me. "And you? You don't await this miracle?"

"No. I'm afraid I haven't time for miracles. Or the heart, anymore."

"It is always good to believe."

"It's also good to get to the task and try to make things happen yourself. Isn't it?"

"A little of both is the answer, I think," he said. And then he went back to his work, measuring.

"My father always said a person makes his own luck." I shocked myself as those words came off my tongue. I had not spoken to anyone of my father since he left me.

"Your father must be a good man."

I blushed. "He lost an arm in the war. But he can do most everything with one arm. Only he left me here and went on to Colorado."

"And you are sad to be left."

"I'm angry. He didn't even say good-bye. He sneaked off in the middle of the night."

The carpenter was wiping some wood he'd taken out of the tub, rubbing it tenderly. And for a moment he did not answer. I felt embarrassed.

"I'm sorry," I said. "I shouldn't have told you that."

He nodded slowly. "The most difficult thing in the world is to be a parent."

"Are you a father?"

"I had a child. Yes."

"Where is he now?"

"Soon we must let our children go," he said. "To find their way in the world. This is more difficult even than being a parent."

He spoke in riddles, it seemed. Well, he was old. Old people do that. Look at Mrs. Lacey. Anyway, I couldn't linger. I told him if there was anything he needed, he should ask me. "I feel responsible for you," I said, "because I brought you here."

He smiled and said what needs he had were few.

I left him there with his tubs of wood and his candlelight. As much as I hated the other girls for what they were doing, going to the Bishop to have the beggar man removed, he worried me. He could never make that staircase. One man with three tools? He needed a helper. He needed better lighting and more tools. Perhaps I shouldn't have brought him here. Still, I hoped the Bishop wouldn't dismiss him. At least he was trying. Nobody else had come up with a solution, had they?

Saint Joseph, indeed. I rushed down the hall. I had some letters to write.

13

❖

THEY WOULDN'T LET ME in to see Delvina, either. The nuns barred my way. One guarded the door of the small sickroom while others rushed in and out with piles of soiled linen and basins of hot water, murmuring, "Not now, not now."

I stood there stupidly with the soft, warm shawl, so delicate in weave and color that it looked like an angel's wing. As Sister Catherine came out I glimpsed the scene inside. Sister Roberta was taking the baby from Delvina and saying something to her in Spanish. *"La veremos dentro de poco."*

Sister Catherine went back in. I handed the shawl to her. She nodded and took it, and I went to my room. When the door closed behind Sister Catherine, I heard the nuns praying.

I POSTED TWO LETTERS on my way to Fort Marcy that afternoon:

Dear Uncle William:
I am sending this to Fort Bent because there is every likeli-

hood that is where you are. By now Daddy has written to you of my dear mama's death. Oh, Uncle William, how I wish I were with you at home in Independence, instead of languishing here in this terrible place.

I know you mourn Mama, but let me tell you, mourning does not help. It only makes the spirit more destitute. If it did help, I would stand at the topmost part of Fort Marcy here in Santa Fe and howl my grief out like a wolf. As it is I cry every night in chapel, and when I am finished crying I still have the miseries, only worse. I don't know how to remedy the situation. And I am surrounded by Catholics who talk only about "offering it up," like Mama's death was some kind of an Indian sacrifice.

They do not understand, of course, all these prissy little girls and nuns. How could they? They surround themselves with reminders of death, in their statues. Their dead saints are all bleeding and suffering. And since Mama wasn't eaten by lions or beheaded, with her head put on a platter like Saint John the Baptist, they likely think her death not important, I suppose.

I hate them all. Except maybe Sister Roberta, who takes up for me when I get into trouble, who listens to me when I talk, and hikes up her skirts to ride a horse, and her sleeves to work with her plants. At least she is a human being and a friend.

Elinora, the Bishop's niece, was disagreeable on the whole trip and continues to be a plague to me here. Although her uncle, the Bishop, is a kindly and dear man, he can be more stern than you when provoked. I have another friend here, too. Her name is Mrs. Lacey, and she lost her son in the war. One of my chores each day is to go with her to the cemetery at Fort Marcy to visit her son's grave. She is very wealthy and has given money for the construction of their new chapel, and so the nuns take care of her and abide her peculiarities. But she is crazy as a hooty owl, Uncle William. Yet I regard her in great esteem and betimes think her the most sane one here. This afternoon she is sickly, so I am to make the trip to the cemetery for her. Fort Marcy is like no fort you have ever seen. It is on the wane, in ruins and very spooky. But I like to go there just the same.

Did Daddy write to you since that time on the Trail? Did he tell you how he ran off in the middle of the night and left me without even saying good-bye? I cried so. And I have not heard from him since and probably won't ever again. But I don't care. I want to come home, Uncle William. If you make arrangements for me to do so, I can live in the house in Independence and run it for you. I know how. I am growing up by leaps and bounds. I have all kinds of chores here, which I carry out diligently, and am doing well with my lessons.

I am sorry to write to you with such a sad catalog of concerns. I know you do not want me to be pouting and complaining. I have some projects here now that I must see through, of course, but which will be brought to a conclusion soon, so if you could find it in your heart to send for me, I would be ready. There are wagons leaving here all the time to go back north. I am sure the nuns could find me a good family to travel with.

Ben is very healthy, and I ride him every day, but he doesn't get the chance to run much. The Bishop has offered me a kitten, since I miss my cats so, and I think I shall accept his offer. I have never forgotten what you taught me, Uncle William. I have seized many an argument by the tail and acted with righteous indignation when caught in the wrong. And it did rock people off their feet, especially Mother Magdalena.

Oh, Uncle William, I wish you could meet Mother Magdalena. You need to be loaded for bear to go up against her. Also,

I have tried to keep my anger, like a fire in the wind. Because it is safer than feeling anything else. It keeps me strong.

I cannot conclude this without earnestly entreating you not to think me deficient in courage or spirit because I wish to come home. Please write to me soon.

Affectionately, your loving niece,
Lizzy

Dear Cassie:

You must think me a very fickle friend, indeed, for not writing, but I have scarce had a moment since Daddy left me at this school in Santa Fe. I suppose that if you saw Uncle William at all and inquired after me you know that. Oh, Cassie, I miss you so! I miss my school and our afternoon rides, with me on Ben and you on Susie. That world seems so far away now—it is as if I never walked the streets of Independence, and it is the only home I have known before this.

Yes, my dear mama is dead. Do you remember how we'd come in from our afternoon rides and she'd have fresh muffins and warm cocoa for us in the cold weather? Oh, I long for her. Be good to your own mama, Cassie, no matter how stern she gets when you forget to do your chores.

I suppose she will soon have the baby. Oh, you are so lucky! There was a new baby just born here in Santa Fe, and I got to know the woman. She had it alone, at the fort, and we brought her and the baby back. She ran from her husband because he beats her. And now she may be dying. How can people not appreciate what they have, Cassie?

Sometimes I think if I can close my eyes, I can be back in our kitchen in Independence, and my own mama will be there. It seems impossible to think of her gone. Where is she? I know I am supposed to think she is in heaven, but how can she be when she is so needed here? My daddy will never be able to carry on alone, little as I care about him, and surely I will become even more of a ruffian without her.

I am already well on my way here in this convent, surrounded by lily-livered girls whose every dream is to see visions of Saint Joseph or the Virgin. Elinora turned out to be as much of a plague as you said she would be and now says she wants to be a nun. But I know she is doing it for her own ends, which I cannot explain now but will tell you in the future.

The school principal is Mother Magdalena, who is mean and unfair and often at odds with the Bishop. She already switched me for something I did not do. But I have a friend in the Bishop. He has a beautiful white cat that just had kittens, and he offered me one. And I have another friend in Mrs. Lacey, an elderly lady it is my job to help care for.

I still ride Ben every day. I haven't time now to explain it all, only to say please forgive my tardiness in not writing and know that I think of you all the time. How are my cats? I know you are taking good care of them for me. I miss them so.

Cassie, because I don't know if I shall ever hear from Daddy again, I have written to ask Uncle William to send for me. I am sure I will be back in Independence next summer.

I must finish now because I have a pressing chore this afternoon. I will write again soon.

Your ever dear friend,
Lizzy

14

❖

I RODE BEN QUIETLY through town. It was cold now, though when the sun came out from behind the clouds, it was warm. Inside the pocket of my apron, I had the note for Jesse James.

How pointless. There was no Jesse James loitering about Fort Marcy. He loitered only in Mrs. Lacey's imagination. I was not so sure about Lozen, though. If she hadn't delivered Delvina's baby, who had?

I also had a new candle and matches to light the lantern beside Robert's grave.

It seemed a silly mission, but I could not refuse Mrs. Lacey. And it afforded me my ride on Ben and an hour or so of freedom away from the school.

Since I had just dispatched letters to them, I thought about Uncle William and Cassie as we climbed the hill to the old fort, which seemed more stark and abandoned on this cold day. Wind whistled around the crumbled buildings. I made my way directly to Robert's grave, got off Ben, retrieved the matches and candle from my sack, then the note for Jesse James from my pocket. I set the note under a rock so it wouldn't fly away. I knelt down to put a new candle in the lantern.

All I recollect is a rush, as of wind, coming toward me. Only it wasn't wind, it was a person, come out of nowhere, a person who came like a dark wind. I remember a cloak flapping in the wind, and then that cloak seemed to envelope me as someone grabbed me by the shoulders.

"Where is she? Where is my wife?"

The voice was gravelly. Strong hands held my shoulders until they hurt. Then he pulled me to my feet. The matches and candle fell from my hands. I heard the lantern clatter over and roll away. The man's head was covered with some sort of old flappy hat. His eyes were red rimmed, his face bewhiskered. His mustache drooped, and it had spittle on it.

"My wife! Where have they taken her?"

"Let me go!"

"You know! So does that old harpy who comes here every day. Where are my wife and baby?"

I kicked and screamed. Fear cut through me. He was shaking me, dragging me, bellowing at me. I smelled the stench of liquor on his breath.

"Tell me, or I'll kill you here and now, girl!"

I fought and kicked and yelled. Then I thought he was releasing me, for he let go of one of my shoulders, but it was only to take a knife from his belt. It flashed in the weak sunlight. "Now! Or I'll kill you!"

At that moment, a shot rang out and I thought I was dead, but instead his mouth formed a large O, and I saw he had rotten teeth. His eyes seemed to bulge and his other hand fell from my shoulder. That is all I remember. Except hitting the ground. Hard.

When I awoke it was to Ben nuzzling my face, pushing me. I struggled to sit up and look around. For a moment I was so dazed that I could not determine where I was or what had happened. My head hurt and my shoulders, too. That made me remember, and I looked around in terror.

The man was gone. But on some stones near me there was blood. And there were scuffle marks in the sand, as if someone had dragged something. The lantern was set to rights at Robert's grave, the new candle lit inside and the matches left near it.

The note to Jesse James that I'd left under the rock was gone.

Ben was still nuzzling me.

"All right," I told him. "I'm all right." I got to my feet and leaned against him for a moment.

Someone had rescued me. But who? I was trembling with fear and exhaustion from fighting that loathsome man. No wonder Delvina had taken refuge up here rather than live with him. But who had come to my rescue? And why hadn't he, or she, waited until I came to so I could give my proper thanks?

I cast my gaze around the deserted fort, feeling eyes upon me. The place was downright creepy, but I would not be frightened off. I patted Ben's nose and, just in case anyone was watching, I knelt down by Robert's grave as if to say a prayer. Then, taking my time, I gathered my cloak around me and mounted Ben and started slowly down the hill.

"It's all right, Ben," I told him again, for I could see he was agitated. His ears were back and he neighed restlessly. In a moment I becalmed him.

"Do you think Delvina's husband is dead?" I asked him.

"That he was shot and dragged away?" I kept looking back as we descended the hill, but saw nothing.

"Was it Lozen who rescued me, Ben? Or Jesse James? And who took the note?"

But Ben kept his own counsel, as he always did.

"Likely it was a lawman," I said. "And likely Delvina's husband is sitting in jail right this minute."

We made our way down the hill and home to the convent. "You know what, Ben?" I said. "I don't think I should tell anybody about this. Because then Mother Magdalena might convince the Bishop to put Delvina out. And she won't let me come here anymore. And that will end my afternoon rides with you."

He agreed.

My teeth were chattering, but it wasn't that cold. As we proceeded home I thought, *I've been here a little over one week, and I've been attacked, whipped, abandoned, lied to, confided in, put under a spell by a witch, put into a penance chamber, slept in a feather bed, been blessed by a bishop, and offered a cat. Who knows what will happen before spring, when I start my trip back to Independence?*

JUST AS I PASSED the U.S. Army quartermaster's depot, a boy ran out of an alley and seized Ben's reins. "Are you Lizzy Enders? Stop, please! I have something for you to give to Elinora St. Clair."

He was so handsome. Never in all my life had I laid eyes on such a handsome boy.

At first Ben was frightened. He reared, but I managed to gentle him. Handsome or not, the boy was a fool. "You stupid bounder!" I yelled at the boy. "You don't ever run out of an alley and frighten a horse like that! What ails you?"

"I am so sorry, *señorita.*" He took off his hat and bowed. He had a head of curly brown hair. *Oh Cassie,* I thought, *he's even more handsome than Charlie Walters in the sixth grade. Remember how smitten you were with him?*

I slipped off Ben's back. "What do you want? Who are you?"

"Abeyta," he said.

"Abeyta what?"

"No matter, *señorita.*" Then he leaned over and kissed my hand. "My apologies for frightening you. But someone saw you go up to the fort before, and I waited until your return. Forgive me."

I'd never had my hand kissed before. I drew it back. It felt like I was branded. "What do you want of me?"

"I would prevail upon you to give this note to Elinora." He held out a folded piece of parchment.

Was this all I was good for? Delivering notes this day? "How do you know Elinora?"

"*Señorita.* I go to the boys school. Over there." He pointed to the distance, beyond the famous wall. "Did Elinora not tell you of me?"

"No," I said. "Though she did make mention of sneaking out at night. Are you kin to her?"

It was a cruel question, because I knew he was not. The look in his eyes when he uttered Elinora's name did not bespeak the concern of a relative.

"She has the voice of an angel," he said. "The way she sings, *Madre de Dios.* I sing, too, *señorita.* And we have become soul mates." He looked abashedly at the ground.

All I could think of was, *How does a girl who is as ugly as Elinora get to have a soul mate who looks like this?*

"We have met four times already, by the wall at the boys

school. This note will remind her. Tonight is the Comanche moon."

"The Comanche moon?"

He nodded. "It is said that if lovers stand very still on the night of the Comanche moon, they will see warriors crossing the river. And hear their chanting. And their war drums. And if this happens, the lovers will be blessed forever and their union will be certain."

I nodded. "But Elinora said only this morning that she is to become a nun."

He laughed, showing perfect white teeth, the sight of which tore into me, broke my heart. "She only says that to throw people off the scent. So they won't suspect about us."

"I never believed it. I thought she was doing it to gain favor with her uncle."

"Which she badly needs. Will you give her the note, please?"

"I'll take it," I said. And I did. "But this could bring great tribulation to you, and to the Bishop. It would hurt him so if he knew Elinora has taken up with a young man. The Bishop has been good to me."

He bowed again. "Do what is in your heart, *señorita,*" he said. Then he turned to go.

"Wait," I said. "Aren't you afraid of what will happen to you if you are caught?"

"We will not be caught. Anyway, my father is Manuel Antonio Chaves, an important personage hereabouts. Ask anyone about him. He gives much money to the church."

Like Mrs. Lacey, I thought. *And like Mrs. Lacey, he likely gets away with all kinds of mischief. And so would his son.*

"Are you and Elinora lovers then?" I asked boldly.

He held himself straight and tall. "I shall love her forever.

I would die for her. And one day soon we will make our way out of here on horseback at night and wed."

And we were here only a little more than a week. Then I remembered—Elinora's mother had run off at sixteen. I nodded, put the note in my apron pocket, and got back on Ben. "I will study on the matter," I said again.

Elinora, with her big nose and her provoking ways. Her talk of being a bride of Christ. Encouraging the others to wait for a miracle. She had sneaked out of our room while I had slept like a newborn babe. How did she do it?

Life wasn't fair, I decided. Not at all.

GOD BROODED ON THE school when I got back late that afternoon. The first thing Ramona told me in her halting English was that Delvina had died.

That sat hard on me, though I knew it was coming. And though I thought I'd never again be so diminished by a death after Mama's.

As befitted a death, there was an eerie cast about the place. I'd never have thought it could get any gloomier than it usually was, but the nuns had given their all to the effort. Candles that were never lit glowed. Mirrors, in short supply to begin with, were covered lest anyone look into one and find that they themselves still existed in the flesh. At every turn I heard prayers being said, saw the girls going about with folded hands and downcast eyes. The nuns were scurrying back and forth with what could only be winding sheets. The church bell was mournfully tolling.

And then I minded something else.

The hammering inside the chapel, which had begun this morning, had stopped.

Had it stopped in honor of Delvina? Or because Elinora had succeeded with the Bishop?

Then I saw her coming down the hall, eyes lowered, hands joined in front of her, lips moving. She was surrounded by her lieutenants. For a moment, as she passed me, she hesitated and gave me a sly smile. And I knew she had succeeded with the Bishop in stopping the carpenter from his work.

I ran from her. As I turned, I almost bumped into Sister Roberta.

"My, you're in a hurry. Didn't you know? All the girls were told to walk softly and pray for Delvina's soul this day. To refrain from chatter and giggling and give something up at supper."

"I didn't know that, Sister. I'm sorry."

As she looked down at me I thought I saw the usual twinkle in her eyes, but I couldn't be sure. "She died a peaceful death. I was with her. The baby will be baptized this evening and cared for here at the convent."

No death was peaceful. How could she say such? But all they did around here was pray for a "happy death." This was the greatest achievement in life, as far as the nuns were concerned. I nodded, saying nothing.

"Now you should go to Mother Magdalena's office. She wishes to see you."

I was in trouble again. I turned to go.

"Lizzy?"

"Yes, Sister?"

"You look as if you've been in a scrape. Is there anything you wish to tell me?"

I minded then how I looked with my disheveled hair, smudged face, and dirty apron. "Not now, Sister. Not yet."

"Well, you know you can come to me anytime. Now I'd suggest you clean up quickly. Change that apron before you appear before Mother Magdalena. Hurry."

I thanked her and ran. Was something wrong? Fear coursed through me as I washed my face, ran a comb through my hair, and changed my apron. Had Mother Magdalena been told by the authorities that I'd been attacked up at the fort? Was she going to forbid me to go out on Ben?

Ten minutes later, I knocked on the door of Mother Magdalena's office and stood before her.

"Sit down, Elizabeth."

I sat. Something bad had happened, I was certain of it. Maybe she had found out about the note I held for Elinora. Hadn't she told me there was little around here she didn't know about?

"What happened to your face, Elizabeth?"

My face hurt by now. I'd fallen harder than I realized. "I fell."

"Where?"

"I tripped in my room," I lied.

She nodded. "You have heard the news about Delvina, I take it."

"Yes, ma'am."

"Since the rules in Santa Fe require that bodies be buried within twenty-four hours, and tomorrow is Sunday, the funeral will be this evening. We are keeping the baby. It is the Bishop's wish, since there seem to be no relatives but a drunken, violent father."

I looked at my folded hands in my lap and nodded. What good to tell her about the man who attacked me? He was likely dead, anyway.

"I have a letter here for you, Elizabeth. From your father."
She handed the missive across the desk to me. I could scarce
move for a moment. My father had written to me? Why? I did
not want his letter. But I got up and took it, fearful that it
would burst into flames in my hands. I held it in my lap and
saw my father's familiar scrawl. "Miss Elizabeth Enders." Oh,
the writing itself burned into me.

"Thank you," I said.

Her eyes were on me. "Some fathers are drunken and abu-
sive," she said. "Some are not."

I nodded yes.

"And I have this for you." Again she reached out, and
again I got up to take what she had in her hand.

It was a gold coin. I looked at it.

"It's a twenty-dollar gold piece," she said. "Delvina gave it
to me when she was dying. She said to give it to you."

A twenty-dollar gold piece! Was there to be no end to this
day and what it would bring me?

This was the gold piece that Mrs. Lacey said had been
given to Delvina by Jesse James.

15

❖

I SAT QUIETLY in my room on my bed, fingering the gold coin. Was it from Jesse James? I was starting to get like Mrs. Lacey, I thought. It was a beautiful coin, and there seemed to be some magic in the thought that it could be from Jesse James. But then I minded that Delvina's husband had been a thief. And likely it was part of some illegal bounty.

I'd been excused from the supper table to read my father's letter. It sat now like some dead thing in my lap.

"Dear Lizzy," he'd written. How could he call me "dear"? He'd left me, abandoned me just when I needed him most, and now he wrote endearments. I'd always thought it was stupid to begin letters by calling the other person "dear."

Men did it to each other in letters about business. I'd seen Uncle William receive letters from some bedraggled, worndown fur trapper, that began with "dear."

My father was on his way to Texas.

At the outset on the Gila Trail, on his way to Colorado, he'd met a drover who worked for the Santa Gertrudis Ranch in Texas, owned by a man named King. The drover had just returned from driving a herd of cattle north, to the Plains. He'd told my father how King needed good men on his ranch, which was the biggest in the Southwest, and how my father, having once run a plantation, would find good-paying work. My father immediately abandoned his Colorado idea and started for Texas.

"Especially, he needs a foreman," my father wrote. "Texas is sending millions of cattle to eastern markets. This man King has six hundred thousand acres and he needs someone to hire and oversee responsible men to take a market-ready herd of some five thousand steers to Kansas. I can earn over five thousand dollars a year."

It was all about money, profits, and the market for cattle.

There was only one line about me, and no sentiments at all about leaving me.

"I know you will do well at school," he ended, "and, after your education, come to live with me at the Santa Gertrudis Ranch. If I get the job, I am to have my own small hacienda."

Tears rolled down my face as I sat with the letter in my lap and wondered what the market would be like, when I was finished with my education, for a daughter who hated her father, yet yearned for him at the same time.

I PUT A SHAWL on and went to the barn to feed Ben his supper. Ben always comforted me. I fed him, and the fragrance of the oats becalmed me. Watching Ben eat did, too. It was such a simple, yet certain act, with no trickery attached to it. Animals had such faith, I decided. More than we humans had. Yet they were so dependent on us. Without our food, our care, they couldn't live. So then, to Ben, I was sort of a god. But he never doubted me.

"Oh, Ben," I told him, "I don't know what to do. Daddy wrote and didn't even say he was sorry he left us. Now he wants me to write back. How can I? And what do I do about the note for Elinora? Do I give it to her or not?"

"Is the coffin all right?"

I turned, startled. He stood there, the carpenter-beggar, eyes hopeful. "I made it in such a hurry for the woman. Is it all right?"

"Yes," I said. "It is fine."

"It is so sad about the woman dying."

"Yes. It seems there's been nothing but death all around since I left Independence."

"It is all around us, always. Every day could be the last for any of us. The trick is to know it, and enjoy each day, even with all its troubles."

"Why did they set you to making a coffin when you have such work on the staircase?" I asked carefully.

"The Bishop has requested I leave off on the staircase for a while. He said some of the girls want to wait, to give Saint Joseph a chance at his miracle. They made a pilgrimage to the Bishop's farm today to lay this request at his feet."

The farm was six miles away. And they'd been driven there by Gregorio. Hardly a pilgrimage. But I kept silent.

"They begged the Bishop to wait at least a week," he went on. "Apparently he thinks he should do this, to give their faith a chance. Also, it seems one of them has a calling to become a nun. And she beseeched him. And he feels, in respect for her calling, he should honor her wishes."

So Elinora had gotten her way in all things, even convincing her uncle that her "calling" was real.

"But then the staircase will never be finished by Christmas. You could not possibly get it done!"

He smiled. "I got a coffin done this afternoon, didn't I?" Then he grew sober. "But waiting idly is not a good idea. I must find other work so I can eat."

"Wouldn't they let you stay on and feed you?"

"I couldn't do that," he said. "I couldn't accept food for nothing, no."

I cast my eyes around the barn, the soft sweetness of the lantern light on the hay, the cows and mules and horses munching. "Oh, I feel so terrible."

"Well," he said, "perhaps Saint Joseph will work his miracle yet. But enough talk of my troubles. *You* seem troubled. I heard you talking to the horse. Perhaps I can help."

I blushed. "I always talk to Ben. He listens."

He nodded. "You heard from your father, then?"

I remembered that I'd told him about Daddy one time in the chapel. And how kind he'd been. Hadn't he said he was a father, too?

"Yes," I allowed. "He wrote to me. But it was a terrible letter. All he talked about was this ranch in Texas where he is going to find work. And how much money he would earn. And the price of cattle. He didn't even say he was sorry for leaving me here. And now he wants me to write to him. And I can't find it in my heart to do so."

Again he nodded. His eyes, which I'd thought of as old, seemed young and hopeful of a sudden. "Fathers always worry about finding work. It is a great burden. Sometimes the work seems more important to the family than they are. It is not so."

What did he know about that? A beggar man. But I did not want to be unkind. "Still, I don't want to write to him," I said.

"He will wait for your letter."

"As I have waited for him here. For him to say he is sorry he had to leave me. But he never said it."

"For some men it is a difficult thing to say. They talk all around it. They wash it over because they don't know what words to put on the hurt they have done."

"Did you hurt your family?"

He sighed. "Only by leaving them."

"You left your family, too?"

"The time came when I had to."

"Nobody ever has to leave if they don't want to," I said. "Not unless they die. Like my mother. And Delvina. I know you are a kind man. And I know I mustn't pry. But how can I write to my father? He'll think I put no store on the fact that he left me."

"He knows what he has done. Fathers always know. And we all carry guilt with us. It's part of being human. Likely he waits for your forgiveness. You don't have to say you forgive him, if you don't wish to. A letter would be enough."

"I don't know," I said haltingly.

"Think on it," he said. "Life is so brief. Often we wait too long to say things."

I nodded, agreeing. "There were things I never got to say to my mother."

"We all have such things inside."

"Yes." I twisted the end of my apron in my lap. "There is something else perhaps you could help me with. Since we're talking."

"Of course," he said.

"But I must swear you to secrecy. You must promise not to tell anyone."

"I promise," he said.

"I have a note here for Elinora. You know Elinora? The Bishop's grandniece?"

"The girl who was with you the night we met."

"Well, I don't know if I should give her the note or not."

"And why is this?"

I looked into his gentle face. His eyes seemed luminous. And encouraging. *He doesn't know Elinora is the one who wants to become a nun,* I thought. *So it's all right to tell him.* "Because it would bring harm to her. You see, it's from a young man from the boys school. He wants her to meet him tonight. He says they've been meeting. I think Elinora is too young for this. Oh, I know I'm not the one to say. But it would hurt her uncle, the Bishop, terribly. And he is such a good man."

He pondered the matter a bit. He sat down on a bale of hay.

"I'm afraid she's going to run away with this young man," I went on. "I wish I myself could tell her to stop seeing him. But she doesn't like me."

"But it would seem that if the contents of the note would do Elinora harm, you should go to someone who would try to keep her from harm."

"I couldn't go to the Bishop," I said. "I wouldn't want to hurt him."

His eyes sought mine. Held mine, as if there was more in the words he was about to say than their meaning. "Then why not give it to Mother Magdalena?" he suggested. "Surely she loves Elinora enough to decide if the Bishop should be told."

It came to me then. Yes! Perfect. Give it to Mother Magdalena! She would tell the Bishop, if even to shove under his nose what his niece was up to.

Furthermore, the Bishop would then know Elinora was lying about being a nun. And he would take back his order about waiting on the staircase.

Oh, I must do it. Quickly. Now. Or we would lose this dear man. "When are you leaving?" I asked.

"Tomorrow night. I must tidy up the chapel before I go."

I thanked him effusively and departed. I am afraid I left him there openmouthed and thinking I lacked in adequate manners. I went out into the night. From the chapel I could hear singing. It drifted out on the cold, clear air. The funeral service was starting. I must attend. I looked up. There in the eastern sky was rising a big balloon of a moon. A Comanche moon.

16

❖

JUST AS I SLIPPED into the back of the church for the funeral mass, the Bishop was making an announcement.

He asked for a volunteer to stay home from the cemetery to mind the baby, who they had christened Elena. I raised my hand. "Good," he said. "Mother Magdalena will be here, in her office, if you need anything."

I knew I must act quickly. In my pocket was the note from Abeyta to Elinora, and I knew that if I did not soon put it into Mother Magdalena's hands, Elinora would slip away from the funeral procession this night to meet Abeyta under the Comanche moon. And quickly forget about being a bride of Christ.

I determined that I would have time after mass. It would take a while for the procession to assemble. But then the fates were with me. Before mass ended, the wet nurse the nuns had hired to feed the baby, Teresa Espinosa, appeared in the doorway holding the child. She had her own newborn at home, I presumed, or she would not be able to nurse this child. Likely she must leave.

Mother Magdalena left her pew, genuflected, and gestured that I should go with her. Eagerly I did so. And out in the hall they handed me the baby.

Little Elena was a cunning babe, with a round lively face and eyes that seemed to look right at you as if she knew what you were thinking.

Go now, those eyes seemed to say. *Don't let anything stop you.*

So as the wet nurse slipped out the door in the church vestibule, Mother Magdalena walked out into the deserted, candlelit hall, and I followed her, the baby a warm, comforting assurance in my arms. "Ma'am?"

She turned. "What is it, Lizzy? Don't feel up to the task?"

I balanced Elena in one arm and fished in my apron pocket for the note. I held it out for her. "I think you ought to see this, ma'am."

She nodded, and I quickly covered the steps between us. She took the note, read it, and peered at me.

"Where did you get this?"

"I don't like betraying a confidence," I said. "It isn't in me."

"I didn't ask you that."

I cuddled Elena, for support. "From Abeyta. He stopped me in the street this afternoon. I didn't know what to do. But I'm afraid for Elinora. Please don't punish her."

"Don't tell me how to do my job, Lizzy."

"No, ma'am."

"Just attend to that baby. She should sleep. Her cradle is in the kitchen, for now, where it is warm. Don't leave her for a second until the other nuns return."

"Yes, ma'am."

She walked past me, to the church door. She opened it and

went inside. I hurried to the kitchen, where I found Ramona punching some dough for bread, which would be left to rise overnight. I set Elena in her cradle, smiled at Ramona, and went to peek out the door into the hallway.

The funeral procession was coming down the hall. First came the Bishop with his oversize crucifix, then the altar boys with lit candles. Then the pallbearers, one of whom was Gregorio, carrying Delvina's closed coffin. Next came the members of the congregation. All were carrying small lit candles, eager to see the ceremony through, eager to go to the cemetery. I thought it morbid. But these people fed on such things.

At the end of the procession were the nuns. As they closed the door to the chapel, I saw a protesting Elinora, led by Mother Magdalena.

The others filed out the front of the convent into the night of the Comanche moon. Elinora was pulled by Mother Magdalena into her office, and the door closed with a menacing thud.

IN THE MIDDLE OF all the confusion of the past two days, I had a pleasant thing happen to me. When the Bishop went to his farm, Sister Roberta had allowed me into his study to pick out my kitten.

There were four kittens, all soft as down; all with tiny mewing, helpless voices; all cuddled in my hands when I held them. It was a very difficult choice, especially since I could scarce tell them apart.

But there was one with a small bit of amber color on its left paw. It was the most cunning thing, that kitten. I chose it for my very own, and on that night of the funeral took it to my room with me for the first time. I cuddled it in my bed. It was so warm and fluffy, and the way it purred reminded me so of my own cats that I have to confess, I betrayed the Cheyenne and Blackfoot part of me and cried.

I named it Cleo, since it was a girl. I knew my Cleo back in Independence wouldn't mind a bit. Might be she'd even feel flattered. "When I go back to Independence, I'm taking you with me," I told her. She understood. She even licked my nose with her warm, rough tongue.

I FELL IN LOVE with Elena that night. She was so small and helpless. I pretended she was my little sister. Or at least Cassie's. The next morning, after I took Mrs. Lacey her breakfast, I went into the kitchen to visit the child before having my own repast. I knew the wet nurse would be there nursing her. I was right. She sat in a far corner with Elena in her arms.

But I was unprepared for the sight that greeted me.

I found Sister Roberta kneeling on the floor with Ramona. The kitchen table had collapsed and there was flour, and dishes and even broken eggs, all over the place. "I told you this was going to happen one of these days," Sister Roberta was saying. "Now we must have a new table. But somehow, until we get one, this one must be repaired. Lizzy?" She looked up at me. "Come help."

I set myself to the task. It took half an hour. We swept, we wiped, we gathered, we salvaged—parts of Ramona's bread dough, assorted sliced vegetables, a whole bunch of fresh trout Sister had just purchased from a man who came to the door.

"It was the trout," Sister Roberta said. "The minute I put

them on the table, it collapsed. I knew I shouldn't have done that. What do we do now? Oh, I have been telling the Bishop for months that this kitchen is in serious disrepair. Where is the carpenter? Go fetch him, Lizzy. We must have this table repaired if we are to put a noon meal on the table."

I stood dumbly, full of flour. It was on my hands, my face, my purple uniform. *If there is any kind of a miracle around here to believe in,* I told myself, *it is happening right here and right now. That this table should collapse at this moment, that the carpenter should be needed just as he was dismissed—it has happened for some reason.*

But did miracles involve broken table legs, eggs smeared on the floor, flour in one's hair, and smelly fish? Where was the music? Certainly I didn't expect "Panis Angelicus," but wouldn't a few hosannas be in order?

What was wrong with me? I didn't hold with such nonsense, and now I was starting to think like all the rest of them around here.

"Well?" Sister Roberta said. "Don't stand there like the town half-wit. Go fetch José."

"José?"

"Have you suddenly been struck dumb? The carpenter's name is José. And I know, I know, it's the Sabbath, but I'm sure the Lord will forgive him if he repairs our table this day."

Strange. I had never asked his name, and he had never offered it. "It isn't that, Sister."

"Well, what is it, then?"

"He is planning on leaving us tonight."

"Why?"

"Because the Bishop made him stop his work on the staircase for a week, lest Saint Joseph be offended. I don't know if he'll do this."

She raised her eyes to the ceiling. "This is a table. I'm sure Saint Joseph won't mind."

My mind was working fast. I looked around the kitchen, which so badly needed fixing. "Sister."

"I can't hold this trout any longer, Lizzy. Fetch me that basin."

I fetched it. "Sister, the carpenter says he can't wait out the week while Saint Joseph decides to come, because he can't take food and lodging for nothing."

She dropped the trout into the basin with a loud plop. "Then let him come and work for his food and lodging."

"That's just it, Sister. You gave me an idea."

She walked the basin of trout over to the wooden sink. "Heaven forbid, you've enough ideas of your own."

"If you had other jobs to do, he could stay. I mean, look at this kitchen."

Sister Roberta stood looking while she wiped her hands on a towel.

"The window frames need repairing," I told her. "How often have I heard Ramona saying the rain was leaking in? Right, Ramona?"

"*Si*," she said.

"Ramona is getting a new stove soon. What good, what good, when the kitchen is falling down around our ears? Sister, you've got enough work in this room alone to keep him busy for a month."

She studied for a moment on the matter. "Right now I

need the table fixed. Later I'll take up the matter with the Bishop. Go now, fetch him."

THE RESULT OF ALL this was that I missed Sunday morning breakfast with the others and the carpenter stayed on. He came right to the kitchen with his tools, and while I sat in a corner and drank Ramona's special coffee—sweet with lots of sugar—and ate her corn bread and some eggs, he repaired the table leg. It was not a simple task, because the leg was rotted away. He had to carve a new one and it took most of the morning. I left him there, working.

The noon meal was delayed an hour, but the trout was cooked to perfection and served with Ramona's special browned potatoes.

There were several long tables in the dining room to serve all the girls the noon meal during the week. On weekends we boarders all sat at one table, which was set with a fine linen cloth.

When I went to take my place for the noon meal with the other girls, I saw my dishes and cup had been set away from them, at the end.

Nobody looked at me when I entered and stood next to my place setting. "Do I have the pox?" I asked.

"We don't break bread with a traitor," Lucy said.

Elinora's head was bowed, but I could still see that her face was tear streaked. And I knew then that Mother Magdalena had visited the full extent of her fury on the girl. I almost felt sorry for her.

"I am not a traitor," I said.

"You snitched on your roommate!" I thought Consuello

would leap out of the chair and attack me. Indeed, Winona had to hold her back.

"Stop." Winona stood up. She was a tall girl with two black braids that she wore tipped with bright red ribbons. Her spectacles sat on the end of her nose, giving her an air of authority. "We do not wish to upset Elinora any more. She is beset enough, since her uncle-the-Bishop was told of the note and confined her to house arrest."

"House arrest?" I asked. It had a menacing and legal sound to it.

"She is not allowed to leave the house at all now," Winona recited. "Besides which, he seriously questioned her intention to become a nun, a fact that has made her distraught. How can she have a calling, he asked, when she is meeting a boy nights?"

"My thoughts exactly," I said.

"Not being of the Faith, of course, you cannot understand the ways of Catholics. We do not expect you to," Winona said.

"Why don't you explain it to me, then?"

She sighed and commenced in a patient voice. "Tradition has it that the most popular girls become nuns. The girls who have already formed friendships, not only with other girls but with boys their own age. If you were God, would you want a recluse? Someone who stayed to herself and brooded? Or would you want someone lively and fun-loving, like Elinora?"

Was I expected to answer this question? I was. I sighed. "I can't speak for God," I said, "but I don't think I'd want somebody who sneaked out at night to meet with a boy, no."

"Oh, you jealous little viper. You Yankee!" Winona hissed.

"She's not a Yankee," said Consuello. "Her father kept

slaves. He beat those poor people. And starved them and worked them to death."

"You slaver!" Winona said then.

"I never knew any slaves," I said. "That was all before I was born. But I know my father never beat or starved anybody."

"Abeyta comes from a family of quality hereabouts. He wishes to marry Elinora." Winona had brushed my thought aside.

"Then how can she become a nun?" I asked innocently.

Another thought brushed aside. "Because of your jealousy of Elinora, you have intervened in her friendship with Abeyta. He waited in vain last night under a Comanche moon. Now the success of their union is uncertain."

I would think so, I thought, *after her uncle got through with her.*

"And you have forced her uncle's hand," Winona continued, "so that he has forbidden her from ever speaking of becoming a nun again. Or doing anything to honor her calling."

Having delivered her speech, she sat down and recommenced eating her breakfast.

I stood, dazed. "You're right about one thing," I said. "I don't understand Catholics."

"Then you should have kept out of it," Rosalyn said. "Can't you see how crushed Elinora is that her calling has been so ignored by the Bishop? She suffers the pains of a martyr."

"I think she suffers the pains of a scolding by her uncle for sneaking out and meeting a boy," I said.

"How dare you?" Consuello leaped out of her chair this time. And what with the impediment of her weight, which was considerable, this was no mean feat. "Even if Elinora didn't have a calling, how dare you turn on your schoolmates and be such a snitch? Don't you have any loyalty?"

"Yankees don't have any loyalty," Winona reminded her.

"Neither do slavers," said Rosalyn.

I stood in silence while Consuello's face wavered before me. *She has a lot of hair on her upper lip,* I thought. *Someday she'll have a real problem with a mustache.* "Please remove yourself," I told her quietly, "so I can sit down and eat."

Her eyes glared with hatred. "Everybody hates a snitch. You have broken Elinora's heart. And on Monday, when the other girls come back, all will be told of what you did. And you will be shunned."

"Get out of my way," I said again.

She went back to her place at the table. Having been branded a Yankee, a slaver, and a traitor all at the same time, I decided I was still hungry and I took my own seat, although I was obliged to get up and help myself to the food, which they'd taken all to their end.

Elinora spoke then, for the first time. "There is another matter no one has mentioned. I feel it incumbent upon me to bring it up."

Everyone turned their attention to her.

"That man has been hammering all morning in the kitchen. I thought he was dismissed by my uncle."

They all looked then at me for an explanation, so I gave it. I told them about the broken table, the repairs needed in the kitchen, and how Sister Roberta had hired the carpenter to work there this week. While everyone awaited Saint Joseph.

Elinora raised her eyes to the ceiling. "Does no one understand? Can I not make myself heard? We must have that filthy beggar carpenter out of this place. I don't care whether he's working in the kitchen or the chapel. How can Saint Joseph come here if we have a carpenter working already? It shows Saint Joseph our lack of faith in him."

There were murmurings, of both agreement and consolation from the other girls.

"You had something to do with this," Elinora said to me then. "Just as you brought Abeyta's note to Mother Magdalena. You are an unbeliever, a heretic. What you have done is bring God's wrath down upon this place. Since that man has come we've had nothing but trouble here. Delvina died, and now this, with my uncle refusing to recognize my calling. That filthy beggar must have been sent by Satan himself. But I don't care what my uncle says. I have a calling. And I shall continue praying to Saint Joseph. And he will come."

"We'll pray with you," Consuello said. "We'd be honored to." And the others agreed.

Emboldened by their heartfelt backing, she gained strength. "But first we must effect the removal of that carpenter. Since I cannot go again to my uncle, we shall institute action. When the other girls come back on Monday, we'll launch a regular fast. We'll fast and pray. We'll only take liquid, but we won't eat a thing until the carpenter is gone. What say you, friends?"

"Yes, yes," they all agreed. They fair jumped up and down in their seats with glee. Then they lowered their voices and started speaking of it among themselves. They started to make plans.

I set myself to eating. The fish was excellent. And then I heard Elinora giggle and say, "If my uncle is spoiling for a fight, he'll get one. He doesn't know who he's gone up against when he has me for an adversary. I'm not my mother, you know. She buckled under his authority. Why do you think she ran away with the first man in trousers who asked her? My uncle drove her away with his stupid rules. Well, there is more than one way to skin a cat."

17

❖

ON SUNDAY AFTERNOONS, lest idle hands act as the devil's workshop, we were required to do handwork in the front parlor for an hour.

We could pick from beadwork or embroidery. Consuello, Lucy, Winona, and Rosalyn, who were from wealthy Mexican families, did beadwork. Elinora and I struggled with embroidery. I was doing a sampler in green and red for Uncle William, which I planned on taking when I went back to Independence. It said HOME SWEET HOME.

The five girls sat a distance away from me, by the window where bright sunshine shone in. At their feet, in the middle of their group of chairs, was the Santa Fe *Republican*. This morning everyone was talking about the man shot in the leg up at the fort, who was later seen struggling through town.

The man's name was Ramon Baca. "Long suspected," the newspaper account read, "of the murder of James L. Collins, government official at the U.S. Depository in Santa Fe, who was shot to death in June of 1869, at which time one hundred thousand dollars of government funds, slated to be dispersed to federal office holders and the military in town, was stolen."

The paper reported that he had disappeared from sight and was still at large and dangerous.

A thrill of fear ran through me, even as Rosalyn said, "That's Delvina's husband! I heard Mother Magdalena whispering to Sister Catherine this morning that he might come to the convent and demand the baby."

"My uncle will never give the baby to that brigand," Elinora said. Though chastened, she still bragged about her uncle. *The girl never gives up,* I thought. *And she has no loyalties. None whatsoever.*

Well, I decided, that ends the controversy over whether my protector was Jesse James. Even in this cave of a convent, surrounded by plaster saints with glazed eyes and black-robed nuns and the constant talk of an impending miracle, I could not let myself believe that.

If James had shot him, Baca would be dead, not just wounded in the leg. I knew that with a certainty, even while I fingered the gold piece in my apron pocket that Delvina had left for me, which Mrs. Lacey said was given to her by Jesse James.

I sat away from the other girls, near the hearth. In my lap, under my embroidery hoop, was Cleo, playfully swiping at my thread with her paws.

Upon entering the room, the other girls had put their noses in the air and shunned me. Exactly as they had threatened. Now they were supposed to be doing their beadwork, but instead they were whispering. I pretended not to hear. At first it was all about the shooting of Ramon Baca. They were taken with the goriness of it, the drama. Of the fact that Delvina had been wed to such a man.

"I wonder what he did with all that money he stole," Rosalyn mused.

"Maybe it's hidden at the fort," Lucy conjectured.

I looked up. "There is no money buried at the fort. I go there all the time," I said.

Ramona nudged Consuello. "Did you hear something just now?"

"It was likely a gnat in your ear," Consuello told her.

"Maybe we'll get up a party," Lucy suggested, "and go look for the money at the fort."

"When?" Rosalyn asked. "You know what we have planned for this week. We'll have all we can do with fasting and praying to Saint Joseph."

"That's right." Elinora spoke. "Fasting and praying come first. And getting our petition signed tomorrow to give to my uncle."

They started whispering about the petition then.

"We must write it tonight and have everyone sign it to-morrow," Elinora was saying. "And we must fast tonight. Refuse to take food at supper. If anyone has any treats sent from home, hoard them. We don't have to really starve. Just give the appearance of it."

"Will your uncle accept a petition?" Lucy asked.

"He has to," Elinora assured them. "When the other girls stop eating, he'll have a crisis on his hands. Some of these girls are from important families. Their people give money to the school and convent."

My heart was beating like a drum. *Poor Bishop Lamy,* I thought. He might have fixed churches that were in disrepair when he first came to Santa Fe, brought in badly needed priests and organized the diocese of Santa Fe, which took in all of New Mexico, Arizona, and parts of west Texas and Colorado, but he did not know what an adversary he had in his grandniece. I felt sorry for him.

Just then Elinora leaned forward to whisper something in Lucy's ear. Lucy leaned forward, too, and some of the beads fell off her lap and rolled across the floor.

Immediately Cleo jumped off my lap and pounced on them, racing about and scattering them all over the floor.

"Oh! She has a kitten in here! Everyone knows that isn't allowed!" Rosalyn was on her feet in an instant. She picked up Cleo by the back of her neck and suspended her in midair.

"Give her to me!" I stood up.

"No," Elinora ordered. "Hand her over here."

Rosalyn handed Cleo over to her.

"She's mine! The Bishop gave her to me! Give me my cat!"

"Did you hear something?" Elinora asked the other girls.

"A gnat in your ear," said Lucy.

I reached for Cleo but Elinora would not let go. She stood and faced the window, the wriggling, frightened kitten in her arms. I saw her doing something, then I heard Cleo howl. Then in the next minute, while the other girls held me off, Elinora opened the window and threw Cleo out onto the street.

I could hear Cleo outside, meowing in distress.

"You mean, stinking...you, you, hoydens!" I shouted at them. "To take your anger at me out on an innocent kitten!"

"She's lucky," Elinora said. "The next time we'll drop her in the fireplace. Or see to it that she's drowned in a bucket of water."

I ran out of the room, into the hall, and out the front door to try to find Cleo.

I FOUND HER—dirty, frightened, and cold—after a full twenty minutes of searching. She was huddled in an old pipe in the ground. I picked her up.

Blood ran from her eyes.

What had Elinora done to her?

I dabbed at Cleo's eyes and cuddled her and told her how sorry I was. I took her inside and ran with her into the kitchen to find Sister Roberta.

"I'M REASONABLY SURE she's blind."

Sister Roberta handed Cleo back to me in the infirmary, where I'd eventually found her working. She'd examined Cleo extensively, cleaned her, and given her something to quiet her. "She's been poked in both eyes by a sharp object."

I took the shivering kitten and cuddled her close. She nestled into the crook of my neck. "Elinora," I said. "She was doing embroidery and had a needle in her hand. Oh, Sister, how could anybody harm an innocent creature?"

"There are depths in the human soul that should not be fathomed," she said. "Maybe she'd be best put to sleep. I could do it. It would be painless, poor little thing."

"And if she lives?" I asked.

She shrugged. "In the company of an older cat, she could still learn to do cat things."

"I want to keep her," I said. "May I?"

"She's your cat. But you should tell the Bishop."

"How can I, without getting Elinora in trouble?"

"He will find out. You must find a way to tell him first."

"Is there any chance she'll get better?

"There are always miracles."

Somehow I didn't want to hear that word. I took Cleo back to her mother, who would lick her and feed her and comfort her, even as I wished I could go to my own mother for comfort now.

Were they all crazy in this place?

Was there something in the water here in Santa Fe that turned the mind? Why would Saint Joseph come here to make a staircase?

I settled Cleo back with her mother and decided to go seek out the one person who was halfway sane in this whole place, Mrs. Lacey.

MRS. LACEY WAS NOT WELL. When I'd brought her breakfast she had been in the chair by the window, but now she was back in bed again. I decided not to tell her about the letter from my father.

I now brought her afternoon goat's milk. She waved the tray aside.

"Coffee," she said. "Get me coffee, Lizzy. It helps my neuralgia. More than this pillow they give me. Please, child."

I said I would, and left her to go to the kitchen. Ramona had the makings of supper cooking. It smelled delicious. I lifted one big pot lid and peered in.

Hare jardiniere. Ramona's specialty. Everyone's favorite. I saw the carrots and onions floating in their own sauce. Let them try to resist this tonight.

One of the servants stood over that pot, nurturing the sauce. Ramona was making pastry.

"Could I have a cup of coffee, please?" I asked Ramona. "I have a headache."

She was so busy she scarce paid me mind. Just pointed to the pot. I grabbed a cup and filled it, put in plenty of milk and sugar, thanked her, and left the kitchen with my stolen coffee for Mrs. Lacey.

SHE DRANK IT AS if it were an elixir, something to prolong her life, something that actually gave her strength. She sipped it, she inhaled its fragrance, she smacked her lips. "You saved my life, Lizzy. What would I do without you? My neuralgia is vanishing already."

"If it heals you, why won't they let you have it?"

"It's Mother Magdalena's way of punishing me for being Methodist. Sister Roberta allows it, but she sneaks it to me, too. Mother Magdalena says coffee isn't good for me. I'm old, I'm dying, what bad could it do me now?"

"You're not dying," I said.

"Oh yes, I am, Lizzy. By degrees. Every day I feel weaker and weaker. I have pains in my head, my back, my legs. Something is coming at me from all sides. It's all right, dear, I'm old; it's my time to go. And I must endure the pain, I suppose, to pay for my sins."

"What sins?" I said derisively.

She smiled. "I have many. Would you like to hear them?"

"I'm not a priest."

"Wouldn't tell a priest. Wouldn't tell the Bishop. But I'll tell you, so that maybe you can learn from my miseries. That's the only kind of penance I believe in. Well, do you want to hear?"

"All right," I said.

She sighed and leaned her head back on the pillow. "I was not always a good person, Lizzy, if indeed I am good now. I come from the East, you know. From Virginia. Oh, I have long since lost any of the honeyed Virginia tones, but that is where I come from. Richmond. That is where I lived with my first husband and my Robert, when he was a child.

"My first husband was not a good man. He was many years older than I and thought me wanton, because I enjoyed life. He was very religious and ofttimes raised his hand to me."

"Like Delvina's husband?" I asked.

"Yes. Which is why I was so drawn to help Delvina. But in polite society, in Richmond, a proper lady did not run away. And she did not speak of such things. She suffered in silence. Oh, I wanted to leave, but he would not let me take Robert. You see, I had no rights, even to take my child out of such a situation. So I endured it for years and years while I put on a good face and Robert grew up.

"Well, soon Robert was grown—or, at least, fifteen—and tall and handsome. The war had come. Often Robert tried to interfere when my husband raised a hand to me, and he earned himself beatings for doing so."

She paused, unwilling, or unable, for a moment to go on. Then she recommenced talking.

"I loved that child, oh, so much. He was my pride and joy. I thought staying was the right thing to do. For him. If I ran, I'd have to leave him, and I couldn't bring myself to do that. Now I know I should have."

"Like my father left me?" I asked.

"Sometimes it takes courage to leave," she said. "To make a new life for those you love. But I didn't have that courage. I stayed, and one day when Robert was near sixteen, my husband started beating me rather badly. And Robert came to my defense." She fell silent.

"Was that so bad?" I asked. I wasn't even sixteen, and I knew I'd do that for my mother.

"In this instance it was. Robert killed him," she said.

I came alert. I looked at her sharply. "What?"

"He killed him. My husband had drawn a gun to hold Robert off. They fought over the gun. I don't know if it went off accidentally or if Robert shot him on purpose. Does it matter? Robert killed him."

"And then what happened?"

"I sent a trusted servant for Lieutenant Colonel Lacey—I had met him at a social in Richmond and he was a widower and so kind. We— Oh, how shall I say it? It sounds so trite. We fell in love. As much as I could trust the word. But it wasn't on this count that my husband beat me. He had never learned of my alliance with Lieutenant Colonel Lacey."

"And Colonel Lacey told the authorities?" I asked.

"No. He helped Robert out of town on the first train that went north. Then he arranged things so it looked as if my husband had been shot in a brawl in one of the gambling establishments in Richmond. There were many of them. They called them Hells, and my first husband was known for frequenting them. And then I came west with Colonel Lacey."

"And what of Robert?"

"The western posts were anything but comfortable. We lived, for a while, at Fort Filmore in the New Mexico Territory.

Always we feared an invasion of the Confederates from Texas, fearing they would not only capture New Mexico but seize the Colorado mines and even take southern California."

"Your husband was a Union man?" My eyes widened.

She laughed. "He wasn't yet my husband, remember? Oh, he was in spirit, but my husband was dead. Shot by my son. John Lacey took care of me. Back East, in peacetime, it would have been unforgivable. But this was the West, where everyone had a past life, a secret to hide. And wartime broke down so many of the old social rules. I was accepted as his wife. I became Mrs. Colonel John Lacey within six months."

"And what of Robert?"

"He joined the army. I didn't even know it at first. It took us awhile to find out where he was, and that came about only because of Colonel Lacey's efforts and connections. Robert didn't want us to find out, because he was too young to be in the army and he feared Colonel Lacey would effect a dismissal. By the time we located him, he'd been killed. It happened at Ball's Bluff in Virginia in the fall of sixty-one. And when word finally got to us out here, my John used all the power he had as an army officer to have Robert's body dug up and shipped here. It took months. We were at Fort Craig on the Rio Grande then. It was under Colonel Canby. John rode out with Canby and his men to engage Sibley's brigade at Valverde in February of sixty-two. The Confederates won and were marching to take Santa Fe when my boy's body arrived by wagon on the Santa Fe Trail. We buried him here and were ready to flee when we heard that the Confederates were beaten at Glorieta Pass here in New Mexico. John was assigned to stay, so we stayed."

"When did John die?" I asked.

"About eight years ago. We were very happy, but I never forgave myself, Lizzy, never, for what Robert was led to do. I know if I'd left my first husband, he and Robert would never have come to blows."

"Robert may have run off to war anyway, if you'd left," I told her.

I let her cry for a bit. I took the cup from her hands and set it down. "It wasn't your fault," I said.

"It's why I give money to the church," she said tearfully. "It came to me that it was a way to redeem Robert's soul. It's why I want the staircase completed. I know that once it is, my Robert will rest and be forgiven for killing his father and be allowed into heaven."

I said nothing, because there was nothing to say. She believed in her quest, and if it made her feel better, what harm in it?

"Promise me you won't leave this place until the staircase is completed," she said.

I promised.

"Even after I die."

I said yes.

"The Union may have won the war, Lizzy, but nobody ever wins a war. Do you know who wins?"

I said no, I didn't.

"Memory," she said. "And that means both sides lose. Because both sides are forever held hostage by memory."

IT WAS LATE IN the afternoon, but I went to visit Robert's grave because Mrs. Lacey had asked me to. I'm glad I went that day. It got me out of the convent and away from the girls who were set on making my life miserable. I'd discovered since Mama died that Sunday afternoons and evenings worked their own mischief on my soul. In my mind, they were connected somehow with family. And as late afternoon turned into evening, an anguish descended upon me each Sunday to which I could put no name.

I missed everyone. Home seemed like something I could never find again. A hollowness seemed carved out of my soul, an empty place that could never be filled. So I'm glad I went, for myself as well as for Mrs. Lacey. Even though I found myself looking over my shoulder, lest Delvina's husband again try to kill me.

I missed the supper hour. But I wasn't scolded. The Bishop had come, and Mother Magdalena was holed up in his study with him. Ramona said the girls had refused to eat anything.

"My *hare jardiniere*!" She was angry, speaking half in English, half in Spanish. But I got the message. Her supper was gone to waste.

"I'll have some," I said.

"What?"

I held out a bowl. "Please. I'm starved."

"You no like them?" she asked. "You don't fast?"

I said no. I wanted to eat. And so I did. I sat at the kitchen table and spooned every delicious morsel into my mouth, while Ramona continued to bang around and take on in Spanish while the wet nurse held Elena to her breast in a corner by the stove.

It was only after I'd finished and said I wanted to take a bowl to Mrs. Lacey that Ramona dropped the pan in her hand.

It went to the floor with a clatter that sounded through my bones. Her hand went to her mouth.

"I forget to say," she told me. "Mrs. La-cee, she sick. Is why the Bishop is here in first place. He say she may die. He make her baptize."

And that was how I found out that my dear friend Mrs. Lacey was out of her head, into some place where I could not reach her. And her worst fear had come true. She had been baptized Catholic. And by the Bishop himself.

18

"LIZZY, COME IN, SIT DOWN."

The Bishop had summoned me to his study early the next morning. He was wearing his most solemn black mantle, which went with his solemn face, yet he was unerringly polite, even gallant, as he pulled up a chair for me.

I sat.

"How are you faring, Lizzy?"

"Fine, Eminence."

"I know your attachment to Mrs. Lacey. And since she has entrusted herself to your care, I feel it only right that I should tell you I baptized her into the Catholic faith yesterday."

I felt myself blushing. His eyes burned into me. This was a challenge, nothing less. He was a man of honesty, and honesty always hurt. Now he wanted mine in return. Well, I could give him no less, could I?

"She didn't want to be baptized into the Catholic religion. She's Methodist," I said.

"We don't know that she was ever baptized anything. So we want to make sure."

"Make sure of what?"

"Come now, Lizzy. Surely you've been here long enough to know. We want to make sure she goes to heaven."

"Catholic heaven?"

"Is there a difference from a Methodist heaven?"

I felt foolish. "I don't know. I only know she didn't want your baptism. She told me that. She trusted me."

"Lizzy," he said, leaning forward across his desk, "don't you think I should be entrusted with such decisions around here?"

"Yes, Eminence."

"Such a decision is too great a responsibility for a girl your age. And she should not have put it on you. You did your best. You gave to her your friendship, which lightened her final days. It seems to me, Lizzy, that you have more than enough to burden you these days without wondering which heaven Mrs. Lacey will be permitted into. Don't you?"

I looked up, startled, to see the eyes not only burning into me now but sucking the secrets out of me.

"Don't you?" he repeated.

"Yes, Eminence."

"Well, then? Don't you have something to tell me?"

"The kitten you gave me, Eminence. She's been blinded."

"So I have seen. And how did this kitten, that I entrusted to your care, that I told you must be respected as one of God's creatures, become blind? Do you wish to tell me?"'

I wrung my hands together in my lap. "I would tell you, Eminence, but it would get someone else in trouble."

"I would think the one in trouble here is the kitten, Lizzy. She, first, is in trouble. And then you are, because you were responsible for her. Am I to take it that there is a third party in trouble?"

"Yes, Eminence."

"And how is that third party involved?"

"She stuck Cleo in the eyes with her embroidery needle. Because she was angry with me."

He put his elbows on his desk and made a peak with his slender hands. "I would have a name, please, Lizzy." He did not seem surprised. His voice was level and kind. *I suppose, I thought, this man has seen and heard just about everything by now.*

"Will she be punished?"

"I would have a name, please, Lizzy."

"Elinora, Your Eminence." Why was it so difficult to give him the name when I hated her so for what she'd done to the kitten?

He nodded and sighed. He took his elbows off the desk and leaned back in his chair. "Thank you," he said. "You may go now, Lizzy." He picked up some papers and shuffled them on his desk.

I got up to flee. As I reached the door, his voice stopped me. "Lizzy, I hear the girls are shunning you. May I ask why?"

My legs were shaking. "Because I told on Elinora about the note from Abeyta."

His face never changed. "Ah, yes. Well, as I said before, you have enough to burden you. Go have your breakfast, and leave Mrs. Lacey to God."

"Yes, Eminence." I made a quick curtsy and ran from the room. I fled to the dining room, although that was like fleeing to the devil's frying pan.

———

I SAW IMMEDIATELY that the five girls who boarded were eating nothing. They were drinking tea. But they stubbornly refused the fresh fish, eggs, and *pan de maiz.*

When I walked in, Mother Magdalena was standing over them. "I insist that you eat. This cannot go on."

But it was going on. All sat with their hands in their laps, their spines rigid against the chair backs, and their eyes downcast. Elinora was wearing a black lace mantilla on her head. Her lips moved in prayer. Winona couldn't keep her eyes off the platters of food. Rosalyn looked about to cry, and Lucy and Consuello focused their eyes on Elinora from time to time, as if to draw strength from her.

Elinora spoke. "With all due respect, Mother, copies of our petition are even now being circulated among the other girls as they gather in classrooms. By noontime nobody will be eating. Unless my uncle-the-Bishop heeds our request."

"You dare to threaten the Bishop?" Mother Magdalena asked.

Elinora raised her eyes. "No, we do not threaten. We *ask.* That he stop the carpenter from all work this week and let Saint Joseph come and aid us."

"And you know that Saint Joseph won't come if the carpenter works, I suppose." Mother Magdalena's voice was rich with sarcasm.

"Yes, Mother, I know," Elinora replied placidly. "I have a calling, remember. And being that God called me just this week, I don't think it is beyond imagining to believe that Saint Joseph spoke to me. Do you?"

"The only calling you had," Mother Magdalena said sternly, "was the note from Abeyta, summoning you to meet him under the Comanche moon. Now I want you all to stop this ridiculous behavior and eat some food."

"We will not eat," Elinora said. "Even as I speak now, that carpenter is hammering away in the kitchen. How do you think Saint Joseph feels?"

"I don't know how Saint Joseph feels," Mother Magdalena replied, "but I know how you are going to feel shortly if you don't stop this nonsense." She looked at me then, standing at the other end of the table. Her eyes went over me, then the table setting.

"Do you consider yourself too good to sit at this end of the table with the other boarders? Who spoke to you? The Virgin Mary?"

"No, ma'am. Nobody spoke to me. I don't hold with such. I sit here because I'm not wanted up there."

"And why is that, pray?"

"Because she is a snitch and a turncoat," Elinora said. "Because she gave you the note. We have chosen to shun her."

"I see." Mother Magdalena rattled her rosary beads, which hung at her side. "Am I to take it, then, that you are not part of this action not to eat?"

"Yes, ma'am," I said. "I'm about starved. And I intend to sit here and eat all I can. Especially the *pan de maiz*. I adore the way Ramona makes it."

"We adore only God, Elizabeth." Again she rattled her beads, gave the other girls one last look, and strode from the room.

SOMEHOW I GOT through that day. I attended class because, of course, no excuse was accepted for not doing so.

Somehow, word had already got around to the day boarders about me. And it was the worst kind of word that could spread through a school. I was not to be trusted. I was a snitch. Don't pass any notes in front of me, don't say anything untoward about any of the nuns. Don't speak of assignations with boys from the boys academy. Especially don't speak of meeting anyone outside by the grotto to smoke a *cigarillo.* Lizzy Enders will tell.

Wait until they found out I'd also told about Elinora blinding my cat. I felt the silence, the turned-away heads, the snooty looks of all of my classmates as a slap. So I concentrated on my work and my problem with Mrs. Lacey.

Somehow, in spite of what the Bishop had said, I must keep my promise to her and get the baptism voided. A promise was a promise, after all. That's what I'd been taught.

At the noon meal, nobody but me ate anything. Plates of food sat untouched, although I saw two girls sneak some bread and wrap it in handkerchiefs when Elinora and her cohorts weren't looking. They drank tea, instead. And water.

"Drink lots of water," Elinora directed in a loud voice from her table. "It will fill you up."

Toward the end of the classroom day, Elinora came up to me and smiled viciously. "All the girls in school have signed the petition," she said. "I have engaged the services of a courier to take it to the Bishop at his farm. He will receive it this night. By tomorrow your carpenter will be gone, I promise you."

"He isn't my carpenter," I said.

"You brought him here."

"Only because he was hungry, and needed food and lodging."

"Yes, and he was commissioned to do a staircase. One that only Saint Joseph was supposed to do. And his presence has ruined everything for me, all hope of a miracle."

"It isn't your miracle," I told her. "Everyone prayed for it. Why is it suddenly yours?"

"Because it has become mine. Saint Joseph has spoken to me as part of my calling. It has become all tied in together. Saint Joseph told me he will not come and build our staircase as long as that carpenter is here. Don't you see? My uncle must believe me!"

"I see only that you are starting to believe your own lies," I told her. "I see only that you wish to pull the strings and make your uncle do your bidding, to get back at him for your mother's unpleasant stay here. I see only that you must be the center of attention at all times, Elinora, whether it is through Abeyta or through God. And I feel sorry for you."

As I walked away, I wished I felt as brave as I sounded.

BY THE END of the school day, two girls in my French class swooned and had to be taken to Sister Roberta's sickroom on the first floor. When I passed it on my way to the infirmary, I saw them sitting up on cots, spooning soup into their mouths. Sister Roberta stood over them.

A good time to sneak into the infirmary.

I knew where many of the remedies were—the smelling salts, the cloves for aching teeth, the dry baking soda for burns, the pennyroyal tea for stomach troubles. I pushed past them on the shelf, as well as the puffballs to stop bleeding; the ten-penny nails in bottles of strong vinegar, which made a blood tonic; and the powdered chicken gizzard mixed with clean river sand for ulcers. There, at the end of the shelf, were the small asafetida bags. I lifted one out of the box, but before I could turn I heard Sister Roberta's voice.

"You could have asked me for it. I would have given it to you." Sister Roberta stood in the doorway.

I held the small bag of asafetida, guiltily. "Mrs. Lacey is coughing," I said.

"I didn't notice that earlier. But take it anyway. Do." She went about checking on her plants on the windowsills.

"I hear they are shunning you. How is that working out?"

"I'm all right," I allowed.

Then, as I stepped over the threshold, her voice followed me. "Asafetida doesn't void baptism, you know."

I turned to see her smiling at me. Tears of embarrassment came to my eyes. "How did you know?"

"She made me promise the same thing, that if they baptized her I should hang a bag of asafetida around her neck. I don't know where she ever got such a notion."

"How do you know she isn't right?"

She only shook her head. "Go ahead, do what you have to do."

Still, I stood there, wanting her approval, needing it. "If she believes in something, isn't that enough? Isn't that what they teach around here?"

"And you need to believe in this, I suppose," she said sadly. "That a bag of asafetida will void her baptism."

"I'm doing it for Mrs. Lacey, not for me. I don't need to believe in anything."

"No. I'm sure you don't. That's one way of never being disappointed."

"I've had my disappointments," I told her. And my voice quavered saying it.

"Of course you have. So you're safe now. If Saint Joseph doesn't come, you won't be disappointed. No loss of faith for you. Nothing to worry about."

"Do you think he'll come if the Bishop accepts that petition and makes the carpenter stop working?"

"He has already accepted it."

"What?" I felt as if she'd thrown cold water in my face. "Elinora's petition? After what I had to tell him about the cat?"

"Don't be disappointed in him, Lizzy. He can't have girls fasting and fainting away in class. And for some of these day boarders, the food they eat here is the only decent meal they get all day long. He knows that. Just as he knows that he can't always do what he wants to do. And sometimes must do what he doesn't want to do. It's part of being a bishop."

I studied on her words and nodded.

Then, of a sudden, a smile broke out on her face, a beatific smile, nothing less. "So, you told the Bishop about the cat, then. And that's why Elinora was given a switching."

"Elinora was switched?" I forgot, in an instant, about the petition. "By Mother Magdalena? For blinding my cat?" I couldn't believe it. "But the Bishop told me he didn't believe in corporal punishment. Why did he let Mother Magdalena switch her?"

"He doesn't. But in this case, I hear, he said that going against his principles was the least he could do when the poor cat was left physically harmed. Nothing riles him more than people mistreating animals. He once knocked a man off his feet on the streets of town for beating his donkey. Only Mother Magdalena didn't switch Elinora."

"You, then?" I gaped at her, at once delighted and shamed for that delight. And frightened now of facing Elinora.

"No," she said. "The Bishop isn't a man to let anyone do his dirty work for him. If there's an unpleasant chore, he'll do it himself. Just like he himself told the carpenter to stop work for a week hence."

"Oh." It took me a moment to take in all she was saying. The Bishop switching Elinora. Then accepting her petition. And what it meant. "Then José will leave. And there will be no staircase."

"Be careful there, Lizzy Enders. You sound disappointed. It almost made me think, there for a minute, that you believed in that carpenter."

"He was doing beautiful work. I know he could have finished it for Christmas. It would have made Mrs. Lacey so happy to know he was working on it. And now he's stopped and she . . ." My voice failed me. Despair surged through me. "I wanted that staircase, and I wanted that carpenter to finish it. For Mrs. Lacey!"

"I know, Lizzy." Sister Roberta's voice was tender.

I didn't want tender, however. I could not abide it. I was more accustomed to dealing with adversaries. "Don't be nice to me." I wiped my eyes with my sleeve.

"Oh? And why?"

"Because everybody who's nice to me either dies or leaves. I'd rather we be at cross-purposes."

"I understand," she said quietly. "But I promise, I'm not dying or leaving. So you can believe in me all you want. And if you do, will you listen to a suggestion I have that might get the carpenter to stay?"

I didn't say yes. I didn't say anything. I just looked at her. That in itself gave her permission to continue.

"I've gotten to know him quite well in the time he worked in the kitchen. He told me he came here because you invited him. He came for you. I think he would stay for you, if you asked him."

"Why?" I asked.

"He told me how you two had discussed things." The way she said the word *things* put special meaning on it. I knew immediately what she meant.

"He told me how he hoped he'd influenced you for the best. He's a lonely man, without a family. He had to leave his own family to fend for themselves, he said. I think he would feel as if he made up for some of that if he knew he'd convinced you to write to your father."

I knew she would come around to that sooner or later.

"As a matter of fact, I think if you did write to your father, José would be so happy, he'd stay. Then, if Saint Joseph doesn't come to our aid, why, we'll have José to make the staircase."

"You have no right to ask me that," I said.

"I know, Lizzy."

"I thought you believed in Saint Joseph."

"Oh, I do."

"That makes no sense."

"When you're talking miracles, not much does," she said. "Now take your asafetida and do what you have to do."

I wasn't sure I wanted to do it anymore. But after all, a promise is a promise.

19

Dear Daddy:

How can I call him "dear"? He left me, abandoned me, just when I needed him most. I do not mean the term, but then neither do I mean the letter. I am doing it only to show the carpenter, to make him happy, so maybe he will stay.

I am sending this to the Santa Gertrudis Ranch, as you suggested. I suppose you are there by now. I hope they have given you a job.

I'll wager he hates working for someone else again. I remember how he'd hated being a storekeeper for Uncle William. It must be difficult looking around the biggest ranch in the Southwest and remembering his own plantation. But I can't say that to him, no.

I suppose I am doing fine here if you consider my grades. I am not a number-one student, but I am acquitting myself proudly. That is what Mother Magdalena says, when she isn't scolding me for one thing or another. It is very difficult, of course, being among all these Catholic girls. I am the only Methodist. I must go to their church services and suffer their prayers and in-

180

cense and constant murmurings. For all that, the girls who are my
classmates are no better in deportment than were my classmates
back in Independence. Maybe they are worse.

I have no friend among them. Strangely, my friends are some
adults.

I wonder what his duties are at the ranch. When he sees
drovers roping cows, does he envy their abilities? Is he still refusing to fire a gun? Are any of them veterans of the war, from
either side? If they are Union veterans, will they take orders
from him?

I know you were not happy in Independence, Daddy, so I
hope this is a new beginning for you. What are your quarters
like? Are they commodious? Or mean? I am still rooming with
Elinora, but she has turned out to be even more of a plague than
she was on the trip. I have written to Uncle William, asking him
if I can come back to Independence. After all I have been through
here, which I have not yet had time to disclose to you, I am sure
I could go back to school and keep house for him there, too.

I know you asked me to come and live with you. But you
said "after your education." What does that mean? How long
do you think I will be able to stay here? If you really want me
to come, Daddy, you have to be plain about asking. I could
bring Ben. I'm sure he'd be right at home on a ranch. But that
would depend on whether you really want us, Daddy, and are
not saying it just to appear nice. I have a kitten now, too,
though she's blind. And I'm sure that next summer you'd let
me invite Cassie. But you must not shilly-shally about it, because I will go, first, to Uncle William, if you can't make up
your mind. You must say you really want me, Daddy, for me to
even consider it.

At any rate, Daddy, I am well. I hope you are there at the ranch and not on a cattle drive to the eastern markets, although I understand you could earn a lot of money that way.

Of course, he doesn't want me. He'll be off on cattle drives all the time. Didn't he say a drover could earn over five thousand dollars a year? Why would he want me around, anyway?

I must go now. I hope this gets to you soon. I hope your new position there is going well.

Until I started writing this, I didn't really know how I felt, but oh, I hope you want me!

Your affectionate daughter,
Lizzy

I don't have to mean it. Do I?

20

❖

I WROTE THE LETTER with Cleo in my lap, mewing and burrowing close to me. When I finished, I folded the parchment carefully, put Cleo in my apron pocket, and went to Mrs. Lacey's room. She was sleeping peacefully.

I tied the bag of asafetida around her neck.

Next I stopped in the kitchen, where they had set up Elena's cradle so that she was always in front of someone's eyes. She was sleeping. She looked like a baby doll, lying there in her linen gown and little bonnet. I felt a surge of love for her, for her helplessness. The other girls hadn't paid her any mind, busy as they were with their own personal concerns. But I often picked her up. Tomorrow, Ramona said, I might help bathe her.

I had always wanted a little sister. All of my classmates in Independence had sisters and brothers. I had none. And being an only child was smothering. I had often felt that everything I did either made my parents' happiness or broke it forever.

I leaned over the cradle and kissed Elena, then I went to the barn to seek out José.

I CAME UPON HIM mending his sandals. He sat on a bale of hay. He looked up and smiled at me. "How are you faring?" he asked.

"I was hoping to convince you to stay," I said.

He sighed and gestured that I should sit. "I am not wanted. Knowledge of that is worse even than accepting charity."

"I want you to stay. As for charity, you don't have to take all the money for the staircase, then. You can take some off for this week of food and lodging."

"If only all accounts could be settled so easily," he said.

"Will you stay, then?"

He looked at me. "There is a lot of bad feeling in this place. It is like an undercurrent in the sea. It pulls one under."

"I know." I fished the letter to my father out of my apron pocket. "Here. I've written this to my father. I want you to read it."

He read the letter, taking his time about it, stroking his beard, nodding. And while he read it I looked about the barn and thought how unlikely all this was. Three months ago I'd been in Independence with my mother and father, with a trip to Santa Fe only talk around the table. Now I sat in a barn in Santa Fe, awaiting approval from a carpenter—a stranger—about a letter to my father, who was in the land called Texas, having left me. I was surrounded by Catholics. My mother was dead. I'd just tied a bag of stinking asafetida around the neck of a comatose woman so she could go to her Methodist heaven. In my pocket was a blind kitten, rendered so by girls who were waiting for a visit from a saint.

"It is a good letter," he said.

"Thank you."

"It bodes good feeling."

Just then Cleo meowed and stuck her head out of my pocket. José looked startled at first, then smiled and cupped his hands. I put her into them. "She's blind," I said.

"Born that way?"

"No." Hesitantly I told him what had happened.

His eyes took on depths that seemed to hold all the sadness in the world, not only for the cruelty that had been done to Cleo but to all, man and beast. He stroked Cleo gently. "I thought this was a holy place," he said.

"It is, oh, it is!" I said in a rush of need to suddenly defend the school and convent. "The nuns have taken in Elena, the baby. And they will raise her. The Bishop is such a good man! In all my life I have known no better."

He nodded, holding the kitten up in his hands before his face. He gazed at her, and Cleo, poor little thing, did her best to gaze back.

"Sister Roberta said she might see again someday. What do you think?"

"She might," he said, handing Cleo back to me. "You must love her and care for her well."

"Oh, I will," I promised.

"Now what will you do if your father asks you to come and live with him?" he asked me, picking up a sandal again to work on it.

"Likely I'll go," I said.

"You will?"

"Yes. I'll take Cleo and Ben and...and—" I looked around me in the barn, wanting to include more, wanting to say more, wanting to let him know that we weren't all what he thought around here. Oh, some were. And I was. For I was lying to his face.

"I'll take Elena. Yes, I've been thinking on it. I'll ask Mother Magdalena if I can take baby Elena and give her a home."

He smiled. "You would do all that for me, Lizzy? Just to get me to wait around a week and take food and lodging for nothing?"

I cuddled Cleo close to me. "I always wanted a little sister," I said. But I could not look him full in the face.

"Then I will stay, Lizzy. I will stay the week."

I gasped. "You will?"

"Yes. But you must not feel that you must give the baby a home just for me. That would be something that the heart should be sure of."

"I'm sure." I stood up, clutching Cleo. I felt strange of a sudden. The idea of going to live with my father in Texas and taking Elena had never been in my mind until this moment, until I'd sat down in the carpenter's presence. And now I felt the idea growing inside me, falling into place and beating with regularity. Like a new heart.

"You should have boots," I told José, "like all the other men around here have. Not sandals."

"They have always served my needs," he said.

"You will tell the Bishop, then, that you are staying? Even though you can't go about hammering this week?"

"I will tell him," he promised.

I started to move away, then stopped. "May I ask you something?"

"Of course."

"I know you aren't a religious man. I mean, I never see you praying in the church."

"There are other places to pray," he said. "And even other ways to worship."

"Yes, well, the nuns baptized Mrs. Lacey Catholic before she went into her coma. And she didn't want to be baptized Catholic. She's Methodist, only had no paper to prove her baptism. She knew they would do this and asked me if I would put a bag of asafetida around her neck if they did. Does asafetida void baptism?"

"I have never heard such," he said.

"Then the Catholic baptism will stand?"

"I would think so, yes."

"But what if she is already baptized Methodist? How will God take her? As Methodist or Catholic?"

He paused for a moment in his sewing of the sandal and gazed to a middle distance somewhere behind me. "I think it doesn't matter to God," he said finally. "I think He loves us all the same, Lizzy."

"Would He not take her to heaven because she wanted to void the Catholic baptism?"

He recommenced his sewing. "He is not a punishing God, Lizzy. That is the mistake most people make, thinking He sits with an account book and a big fist, waiting to punish us. He is not a wrathful God but a loving God who made each of us and loved us since we were in our mother's womb. This is only the opinion of a poor, badly educated man, of course, but I think He wants us to enjoy the world as He has given it to us. Else why would He have given us so many beautiful things? Like your kitten, for instance? Or baby Elena?"

Cleo was purring in my arms. I nodded, thanking him. Around me in the barn the animals chomped on their food and a kind of peace descended upon me that made me know everything was going to be all right.

"If Saint Joseph doesn't come, you will finish the staircase for Christmas, won't you?" I asked.

"I will, Lizzy. If Saint Joseph doesn't come."

"They think he's coming," I confided. "Did you ever hear anything so silly?"

He shook his head no and smiled and went right on sewing his sandal.

ELINORA DID NOT COME to our room that night. She spent the night in the penance chamber. I supposed that she would hate me now more than ever. Strange though it was, I had to keep looking at Cleo and reminding myself of what she had done, to be pleased.

21

❖

SAINT JOSEPH DIDN'T COME.

Elinora came back to our room, chastened. "I spent the night with Winona and Lucy," she said. "We had sort of a party to celebrate the success of our petition. I'm so glad my uncle saw the light and agreed to stop the carpenter."

She acted no differently toward me than before. To do so would be to admit she'd been punished. And I didn't flaunt what I knew.

Every morning that following week, she and her lieutenants would rush to the chapel early, before mass, to see if the wondrous staircase had been built. And if the saint had come during the night.

Then there would be long faces and doleful looks at breakfast. Which they dutifully ate because the Bishop had agreed to their demands.

All that stood there in the space where the staircase should be was the affair that José had started. His tubs of water and his wood were gone. So was José.

He was nowhere to be seen. Not on the grounds or in the barn. Even his mule was gone. At first I became frightened, thinking he had left for good. Then on Wednesday of that week, Sister Roberta pulled me aside and told me he was at the Bishop's farm.

I had plenty to distract me from both the staircase and José by then.

On Friday night Mrs. Lacey took a turn for the worse, with a high fever and chills. A doctor was sent for.

"What is this bag doing around her neck?" he asked Sister Roberta.

"It is there to prevent the croup," she said.

"Take it off. You don't have to worry about croup. She won't live until Sunday."

He had the face of a bald chicken. His eyes were so cold with contempt that I felt a draft in the room. And I wondered why they called Jesse James a criminal.

Sister Roberta took the asafetida bag off Mrs. Lacey to please him, then without a word to anyone, put it back on after he left.

"Maybe you shouldn't," I offered. And I told her about the discussion I'd had with the Bishop.

"You hold to your promise," she said. "If the Bishop asks, I'll tell him how she was coughing before she went into a coma."

I loved her even more then. And offered to watch baby Elena after my last class today, to give Sister Roberta some free time. The days still held some warmth in early December, though the nights were frigid. I took Elena, all bundled up in her cradle, out to the garden and sat with her under the arbor.

I had avoided her after I told José that if he stayed I would take her with me to live with my father in Texas. From whence had those words come? It was as if they'd been there inside me all the time, like some kind of an ague, waiting to come out of hiding. Yes, I'd been taken with little Elena since I first laid eyes on her. But only because I'd always wanted a little sister. Those words of mine surprised me as much as they'd surprised José.

So now I offered to watch her again. It was a test for me. I would find out if there was anything behind my words. Certainly I hadn't meant them. Certainly they were said only to convince José to stay. Elena's cunning ways meant nothing to me. I could leave this place tomorrow and never see her again and it wouldn't matter a whit to me. Anyway, the nuns wanted to keep her. And I wasn't going anywhere, as far as I could see. I hadn't even mailed the letter to my father yet.

ELINORA AND I HADN'T really spoken two civil words to each other since she'd been punished for blinding my kitten. We still shared the same room, but I made it my business not to be in it while she was about, fussing with her hair or dressing. There was an hour at night before bed when we were allowed time in our rooms to read or write letters. But I used that hour to see to Elena's bedtime preparations, and usually came in when lights were already out.

Still, that week one had to be blind and a half-wit not to notice Elinora's anxiety. She never sat still for a moment. She giggled incessantly, at nothing. She scarce ate; she tossed continually at night in her bed. And once or twice in the beginning of the week, I had caught her at the window in her nightdress, staring out.

She was going to run away, I decided, because she'd been switched.

The second time I caught her at the window in her night-dress, I sat up in bed. "What are you doing there?" I asked.

She turned from the window. "Just looking out. The night is so fine."

"You're looking for Abeyta, aren't you? Are you to meet him again?"

"Wouldn't you like to know, so you could go and tell Mother Magdalena."

"I don't care this time, Elinora. You could jump out that window right now, and I wouldn't even tell anybody."

In the half-light from the moon, I could sense, rather than see, her sly smile. "Do you really think I'd go before Saint Joseph comes?"

"Is that what you're waiting for? And what if he doesn't come?"

"I'm determined," she said, and she spun around with a dramatic flair, her white nightdress whirling, "that if Saint Joseph comes, I shall become a nun. How can I do anything else? And if he doesn't come, I shall wed Abeyta. I shall take what happens this week as a sign."

I had nothing to direct me, no unworldly compass. Not even a worldly one to tell me what to do. I envied her and her saints and signs in that moment. I truly did.

BUT SAINT JOSEPH did not come.

As the weekend came and went, it was as if I were living in the middle of a tornado, as if the whole student body were already caught up in it and being taken away while I stood there, alone and bereft on the ground, watching them go. In the halls girls walked about with downcast eyes, lips mumbling quiet prayers. They voluntarily kept silence at the table. They bent their heads over their books and chores, never needing chiding or reminding about anything.

But it did no good. Saint Joseph did not come.

ON MONDAY AFTERNOON the day students left the school with downcast spirits and faces, and we settled into a week that I knew would be unbearable, at best. What would Elinora and her lieutenants do now? Would Abeyta come? Would Elinora leave with him?

On Tuesday morning, just as the early light seemed to be reflected back to us from the west, just as the sun was peeping over the Sangre de Cristo Mountains, there came a knock on my bedroom door.

I crept out of bed, shivering in the cold. It was Ramona.

"Sister Roberta, she say come. It is Mrs. La-cee."

"Is she dying?"

"No. She ask for you."

I threw on my robe and, still in bare feet, followed Ramona with her candle, down the stairs, past the plaster saints in their wall crevices, and into Mrs. Lacey's room. She was indeed awake, looking more frail than ever but waiting anxiously for me.

As I knelt beside the bed, she waved the nuns out of the room. The door closed behind us. She took my hand.

"Thank you." Her voice was raspy, and she smiled and gripped the asafetida bag with her other hand. "You are my friend."

"How do you feel?" I asked.

"I'm dying, child. Tell me, is the staircase progressing?"

I lied and said yes. I told her it would be done by Christmas.

"By Christmas I will be in heaven with Robert," she said.

"In Methodist heaven. I'll keep a place for you. But you will have a long life ahead of you before then. I dreamed about you. Do you know what I dreamed? I saw you as the *señora* in a great courtyard, behind a gateway of a rambling adobe house. You own much land, and you keep a hospitable fireside. There were many children about you. But it is not here in New Mexico, but in another vast and enchanting place much like this."

I had not told her of my father's letter, of his invitation to come to Texas. I had not wished to burden her with it.

"Did Saint Joseph ever come?" she asked. Her voice was growing weaker.

"No," I said.

"These Polly Purehearts wouldn't recognize Saint Joseph if he did come." She laughed at her own joke, then coughed. I gave her some water and she drank a few sips. "Lizzy," she said, "do it. Post the letter to your father, child. Do."

Those were the last words she said to me.

She was looking right into my eyes. Right into them, hard. And then her grip loosened on my hands and I leaned over. But I could not weep, because I had wept all the tears out of me for my mother. And there were none yet restored to me. But I felt the pain of her going. In the distance a clock chimed and then wind rattled the windows. There had been no wind, but there now was. I heard it, though I did not feel it. It was rising all around the house, the garden, the walls, the trees, and the street outside, in an upward spiral motion, taking Mrs. Lacey to her Methodist heaven.

LATER THAT DAY, I asked special permission to go to town, which I received from Mother Magdalena. I don't think she would have agreed to let me go—what with the way I looked, which was spent, and the combination of wind wreaking havoc outdoors—except for what I said I wanted to do, when she asked.

She nodded tersely. "Back within the hour, Lizzy. And only one stop. To post your letter."

THE WIND PERSISTED for the better part of that day and into the night. In keeping with the laws of Santa Fe, Mrs. Lacey was to be buried within twenty-four hours.

I kept watch, with Sister Roberta, over her coffin between eight and ten that night in the chapel. Outside, shutters banged and candlelight flickered and the shadows from José's uncompleted staircase reached out across the wall.

At ten o'clock Sister looked up from her prayer book and bade me go to bed. I went to fetch Cleo from her nest with her mother and siblings, and carried her upstairs to sleep with me, as I'd been doing every night now. I fell asleep immediately, numbed and swirling in a vortex of wind-caught voices of memory. It must have been near midnight when I woke. A shutter was banging outside our bedroom window. I sat up.

Elinora was ahead of me, already by the window, drawing a dress over her head. I saw that distinctly in the shadows.

"What are you doing?" I whispered.

She ran back to her bed, knelt down as if to retrieve something from under it, and pulled out her portmanteau. Then she half carried and half dragged it to the window. "It's Abeyta. He's come for me. And I'm going. Don't you dare tell, Lizzy Enders. Abeyta's father is a man of eminence hereabouts, and I promise you will suffer if you try to stop us."

"I wouldn't dream of it," I said.

There was a figure outside the window, and I felt a thrill in spite of myself. Only Elinora would elope in such a romantic way, when she could have met Abeyta in any dozen of ways on the ground. I watched her struggle to push up the window sash. It was a very large window, but she managed.

Then, in the next instant, everything went wrong at once.

The wind rushed in, blowing the curtains about and knocking over with a crash a vase of flowers on a nearby dresser. A figure bounded into the room, got himself entangled in the curtains, grabbed Elinora, clung to her, and they both went tumbling onto the floor, where Elinora promptly started yelling and thrashing about.

"Get off me, you oaf! Who do you think you are?"

It was not, to say the least, Abeyta. But I recognized at once who it was. Ramon Baca, Delvina's brute of a husband. Here, in our very room. In his hand he held a large, ugly knife, while he rolled over Elinora, on the floor. "Where is my baby?" he demanded.

"Who *are* you? How dare you? Where is my Abeyta? What have you done to him?"

Ramon pulled Elinora to her feet, and in the scarce bit of moonlight determined, I suppose, that she was not me. "You are not the one!" he accused.

"I certainly hope not," Elinora cried. Then, "What one?"

"The one who sits in the courtyard with my baby every day." Over her head he looked and saw me, groping the covers around me on my bed like a Sally Sissy. "There. She is the one." He started toward me, but Elinora was more angry than either he or I imagined. And a tornado is easier to confront than an angry, thwarted Elinora.

She held on to his arm. "What did you do to my Abeyta?"

Ramon flung her aside. She toppled and fell but grabbed on to his leg, and he came at me that way, with her clinging to his leg, all across the room, until he turned on her with the knife raised.

It was only then that I bestirred myself, that I lost my fear and leaped from my bed, dumping poor Cleo onto the floor as I grabbed the nearest thing I could take up and smash into his head, as he had the knife raised to stab Elinora. But I didn't do it for Elinora as much as I did it for Elena.

In the dark I did not care what I grabbed. I felt it solid and ominous in my hands, a good weapon. I swung with everything in me, both hands on that weapon. And I hit him in the head and sent him reeling.

At that moment the door of our room opened. Mother Magdalena stood there. Behind her were the other nuns, in nightcaps and nightdresses, as I had never before seen them. And I know our room was never before as they had seen it to be, with the window open and the wind whipping the curtains about, and Elinora cowering there, fully dressed, her portmanteau beside her, and Ramon Baca slumped on the floor, knife still in his hand, his head bleeding.

And me with the bottom half of the Virgin Mary in my hands, the part that stood on the serpent. And the top half in blue and cream-colored bits scattered on the floor.

22

❖

WEDNESDAY MORNING IT SEEMED as if more people than usual came to mass. Some came for Mrs. Lacey's funeral, others to hear what the Bishop would say about Saint Joseph.

At the end of mass the Bishop made his announcement. He told the people that his carpenter, the one he had originally hired, would recommence the stairway that very morning, right after Mrs. Lacey's funeral. Then he said he wanted no more "demonstrations of faith, fasting, starving, or argument."

For a moment he let his gaze sweep over the congregation. "I wish no one to feel that because Saint Joseph did not come to us this week as many believed he would, God has abandoned us," he said. "I owe Him a special thanks this morning for the safety of two of our girls, who were attacked in their room last evening. The attacker has been taken in hand by magistrates and, as we speak, sits in our town jail. So, even as we bury our dear friend and benefactor, Mrs. Lacey, let us turn now to thoughts of readying our hearts for Christmas."

Mrs. Lacey was buried after mass, with all the fanfare and

solemnity of the Catholic Church. We bundled up against the cold, and Mrs. Lacey's coffin was carried on a wagon through the main street of town, through the noisy clatter of the marketplace. By the time we wound up on top of the frozen hill, on the path she and I had taken so many times together, we had a trail of people behind us. People who'd known her and wanted to be part of the burial ceremony.

They put her in the ground on the hill at Fort Marcy, next to her beloved Robert, where she'd insisted on being buried.

The day was cold, and clouds hovered close. The disreputable fort building seemed to be the only thing to hold up the sky on that plateau. It looked as if it might snow any minute.

The grave had been dug and Robert's candle was lit in the lantern. Bishop Lamy himself said the final prayers, while the wind moaned its own dirge. Some of the girls from school looked around nervously at the remnants of the fort. I could tell they felt menaced, as I had the first day I'd seen it. As for me, I looked around and knew, without seeing, that we were all being watched. That after we left the place, people would come out from where they were hidden and go to the grave and smooth the dirt and grieve for Mrs. Lacey.

What people, I could not say. Real or not was not the question. They would be here, not only today but in all the days to come. And that was all that mattered.

As we started down the hill afterward, the Bishop himself came to walk beside me. "Lizzy Enders," he said, "I understand the Virgin herself came to your aid last night."

I found myself blushing. "It was the first thing I grabbed," I said.

"I'm sure she was very happy to be of assistance to you.

God helps those who help themselves, you know. And perhaps that is how we should look at José. Perhaps Saint Joseph sent him. And we need only to let him help us."

"I don't think the girls will accept that, Eminence."

"Likely not. There are miracles all around us that we never see. Every day. How is the kitten?" His eyes smiled down at me.

"She's doing middling well, Eminence."

"Good. I am sure you will give her all the love she needs. Let me thank you properly now for coming to my grandniece's aid. Your courage has shown us all a thing or two about having our hearts in the right places. I am afraid that we Catholics must admit this morning that we do not have the corner on forgiveness."

With that, he put a hand briefly on my shoulder, then quickened his pace to help Elinora maneuver her way back down the hill. As a result of last evening's attack, her forehead sported a purple-and-green lump. And her arm was in a sling. As I watched him tenderly guiding her down the path, I could see how he loved her. And I thought, maybe for the hundredth time, *I love you, Uncle William, but I'd give anything if the Bishop were my uncle.*

I knew I should have told the Bishop that what I'd done was done for baby Elena, not for Elinora. But we Methodists do not have the corner on the need for praise.

BY THE TIME we got back to school, it was near noon and there was a meal in honor of Mrs. Lacey. But it was not solemn, and we were allowed to freely talk at the table. Of a sudden, all the girls wanted to gather around me and Elinora, and we found ourselves thrust together to tell of the adventure last evening.

They wanted to hear about Ramon and the attack. And how I'd hit him with the statue of the Blessed Virgin. Elinora and I found ourselves in places of honor at the table, again thrust together, all animosities forgotten.

I was one of them once more. Forgiven for all my transgressions.

"Lizzy saved my life," Elinora said dramatically. "If not for her, I'd be lying in a coffin next to Mrs. Lacey this day." Only Elinora could deliver such a speech, with such flair, when her arm was in a sling.

Elinora was saying more nice things about me. "I owe you much," she finished.

"You don't owe me anything," I said. "I hate that man. He wants baby Elena. I did it for her."

I caught a glimpse of recognition and appreciation in Elinora's eyes for my lie. "Well, on your way to defending baby Elena, you saved my life. So, please accept my thanks, and let's start over again with our friendship."

We've never had a friendship, I thought. But what could I do? I said yes, and everybody clapped.

MOTHER MAGDALENA CAME into the dining room before we finished our meal, to make an announcement. "Girls," she said, "as much as I dislike doing this, after conferring with the Bishop, we have decided it best, after last night's attack, to find a home for little Elena. We must find a place outside Santa Fe, away from the father who is a criminal. The Bishop does not wish to endanger you all by risking another attack."

"But, Mother," Elinora said, "Ramon Baca is in prison."

"Such men have influence. The man will not long languish in prison," Mother Magdalena said. "So if any of you know of a good family outside Santa Fe, please come to see me in my office. Even if the family is willing to take Elena only for a while, until we can find a permanent home for her."

A pall settled over the table when she left.

After breakfast Elinora came up to me in the hall. "Lizzy, you must learn to accept a compliment," she said. "You are as bristly as a porcupine."

"I haven't had too many friends around here to accept them from," I told her. "In case you haven't noticed."

"I know. We haven't gotten on. I've been beastly to you, haven't I?"

"You blinded my cat."

She stared at me. "I *never,* though I suffered a switching for it. And never did I see my uncle so angry. Not even when he found out about the note from Abeyta. That man gives no quarter to anyone he even suspects of mistreating God's creatures."

"You did, Elinora. Don't deny it."

"Something must have happened to her eyes in the street. Anyway, your cat isn't blind, Lizzy. Didn't you see how she was chasing after the curtains in the room last night?"

"No. How could she see the curtains to chase them?"

"She was," Elinora insisted. "And if you will come with me now, I'll prove to you that she isn't blind."

She was up to something, but I followed her upstairs to our room. Cleo was still nestled in my bed, sleeping. Elinora went to her side of the room, opened a drawer, and pulled out a ball of yarn. "Watch this," she said. Then she unwound the yarn and waved it over Cleo's face.

At once Cleo raised a delicate paw and aimed for the end

of the yarn. Not only that, she followed its progress back and forth with her eyes, which seemed bright and alert again.

"I don't believe it!" I gasped.

"What made you think she was blind?" Elinora asked innocently.

"Blood ran from her eyes that day."

"Lizzy, I admit what I did—throwing her out the window—was mean. But don't forget, you'd just run to Mother Magdalena with a note meant for me. I had to do something."

I picked up Cleo and hugged her. "Take it out on me, then, not on an innocent cat. Anyway, Sister Roberta said she was blind."

"Well, she isn't right about everything." Elinora sat on the bed, next to me. "You must let me make up to you all the bad things I've done, Lizzy. Please, think of something. When my uncle finds out the cat isn't really blind, he'll feel terrible for switching me. And right now he's so happy I wasn't killed last night, he's forgiven me for everything, anyway. Now is the time to ask for anything you want. I can get it for you."

I stared at her. "Elinora, you shouldn't use people so," I said.

She tossed back her hair and gave me a knowing glance. "Oh, but grown-ups do it all the time. It's the way of things, Lizzy. You're still such an innocent. It's time you grew up, isn't it?"

I did not wish to grow up if it meant being like that. But I just shrugged and nodded yes. "Look at this room. It's a mess. We should get to cleaning it," I said, to give the conversation a new turn.

In truth, I was so happy about Cleo that I no longer felt

any anger toward Elinora. So we set ourselves to the task. "Are you still running away with Abeyta?" I asked her while we were cleaning up.

"I want to." She sighed. "I know it seems to you as if I'm frivolous, Lizzy, but Abeyta does love me. And I never wanted to be in this place to begin with. You complain about your father, but do you know why mine sent me here?"

"Because your uncle is the Bishop."

"No. To get shut of me. Because he wants to marry a young woman back in St. Louis, and she doesn't want me around. He hasn't written to me since I've been here. Likely he's married to her already."

I said nothing for a moment. For the first time since I knew her, I felt as if she was telling the truth.

"At least your father has written to you," she said.

"I may go and live with him in Texas," I told her. I couldn't help it. For once I knew I had something she didn't have, and I just could not help it. I told her about the ranch.

"I'd give an arm to live on such a place," she said wistfully.

"My father already has," I told her.

"Oh, forgive me, Lizzy, do. Oh, you must think me terrible."

"Yes. But not for that," I told her. And then we both sat down on the floor and laughed, Cleo between us.

In the silence that followed, she picked up a piece of the Virgin Mary from the floor and held it in her hands. "I was thinking of asking Abeyta's family for help in finding a home for Elena," she said. "They have much influence in this whole territory. What do you think?"

When what I thought came to me, I could scarce speak.

But then I did. "Elinora, I think that if you wish to make up to me for my cat and for other things, I have thought of something," I said.

"A BABY IS NOT a kitten." The Bishop frowned at us severely, standing behind his desk. I was sorry already that Elinora had allowed me to be dragged into this. I did not have the mettle to go up against that frown, the sternness in those eyes. But apparently Elinora did.

"Uncle," she said sweetly, "before we discuss the baby, there is something else we must tell you."

"There is no discussion. You are both dismissed." He sat down and turned his attention to the work on his desk.

I curtsied and started to leave, but Elinora grabbed my arm and pulled me forward. "Lizzy has something to tell you about the kitten." And she dug her nails into my arm until I thought it might well be bleeding, even through my long-sleeved blouse.

He did not look up. "I said you are both dismissed. Don't bring me to anger, Elinora."

The nails dug into my arm harder.

"Eminence," I said. "We have discovered that the kitten is not blind after all. She sees things. She chases them. We thought you'd wish to know."

He looked up. His eyes focused on me in a most disconcerting way. *If you are lying,* they said. *Just let me find out you are lying.*

"Uncle, if you will just permit Lizzy to fetch her from our room, we can prove it. You will see."

He nodded curtly at me. "We will see," he said.

I ran as quickly as I could, and when I returned, breathless, with Cleo in my hands, Elinora was still standing in front of his desk and he was ignoring her, tending to his work. She had removed a ribbon from her thick yellow hair. "Watch, Uncle," she said.

He stood up and came around from his desk as I set Cleo down on the Persian carpet. Then Elinora dangled the ribbon in front of her. Immediately Cleo reached up a delicate paw and tried for it.

"You see, Uncle? I told you."

The Bishop knelt down to pick up Cleo. He held her in his hands and peered into her eyes, then scratched around her ears and set her down. The mother cat had come from her corner to greet her. The Bishop stood up, scratched his chin, and watched Cleo follow her mother across the room. "You are right," he said.

"We just had to tell you," Elinora said sweetly, "because I know how badly you felt because you thought I had blinded her."

He caught himself, frowned again, and went back to sit down. "You mistreated her anyway, Elinora. Only God can forgive that."

"Yes, Uncle," she said sweetly, "but I was punished."

He closed his eyes for a minute, as if praying for strength. Then he sighed. "Very well, Elinora," he said. "You have five minutes."

She plunged right in. "Lizzy's father is getting a job as foreman on one of the biggest ranches in the Southwest. In Texas. Lizzy will someday soon, with your permission, go and live with him. He has asked her. If she could bring the baby there, the child would grow up in an atmosphere of health and love. If she's left anywhere here in New Mexico, Ramon Baca will find her."

He looked at me. "What ranch is this, Lizzy?"

"Santa Gertrudis Ranch, Eminence. The last he wrote, he was likely to get the job running it, like he ran his plantation before the war."

He nodded. "I know Mr. King, who owns the ranch. I was a guest there once."

At Elinora's exclamation of joy, he held up a hand. "This child is under my jurisdiction," he cautioned us. "I will not even consider the matter until I write to Mr. King and to your father, Lizzy, and find out if this plan is agreeable to them. Do you understand?"

We both said yes. Meekly.

"But letters take so long with the mail service," Elinora said. "Perhaps, Uncle, my friend Abeyta can use his father's influence to get a letter immediately to the ranch."

"Abeyta?" Bishop Lamy said.

"Yes, Uncle. He will do it if I ask."

"I have no doubt. Have you seen him lately?"

"No, Uncle."

"The truth, Elinora."

"I haven't, Uncle. I swear. Ask Lizzy. She's seen me in my room every night."

He looked at me.

"She hasn't," I said. Of course, I did not say she intended to elope with Abeyta. For one reason, I decided it was one more of Elinora's dramatic announcements, like being a bride of Christ.

"I will write the letters," the Bishop said, "and send them with Abeyta's father's messenger. And if Mr. King and your father write back and agree, and guarantee me a good home for this child, I will consider it. *If* you both behave. Now you are dismissed."

I had to hand it to Bishop Lamy. He had practically guaranteed Elinora's behavior for months. And she thought *she* was using *him*!

But then he hadn't united the whole of his Southwest flock, started schools where there were none before, and once been in the forefront of defending his wagon train with blazing six-guns from attacking Comanches, for nothing. Certainly it had given him some training to handle his fourteen-year-old grandniece.

Then, as we left the room, I heard him murmur to himself. "Imagine those two coming to me together. I'm beginning to think we did have a miracle here this week after all."

23

✤

IN THE NEXT WEEK everyone seemed to settle down. All
the students were chastened, to say the least, that Saint Joseph
had not come. I myself suspected they also felt a little foolish.

"We have not been worthy of him," Mother Magdalena
told the girls almost every morning at breakfast. "Now Christmas is coming. It is the season of Advent. We must make ourselves worthy of the coming of Jesus."

Thank heavens they didn't really expect Jesus. Even I, a
Methodist, knew that.

From inside the chapel came constant hammering, as José
the carpenter worked on the staircase. He worked long hours,
beginning at six in the morning, stopping for mass, and then
going on until late at night. We were told by Mother Magdalena not to bother him, that he was in a dreadful race against
time to have the staircase completed for Christmas.

I wanted to peek in and say hello, but Mother Magdalena's
order was firm, and things were so tenuous because Saint
Joseph hadn't come and the carpenter was back that I decided
to keep my distance.

The choir practiced for Christmas in the dining room.

Decorations started to appear in the schoolrooms and the convent. Bright wild holly berries, possum haw berries, and evergreens. At the Bishop's farm the boys from the academy were allowed to help with the hog killing.

"Wait until the bonfire on Christmas Eve," one of the day girls told us. "The boys will blow up old hog bladders from last year and throw them on the fire. They explode like cannons."

Ramona was already planning the Christmas Day feast. In the marketplace it seemed as if the trinkets of the world were on sale. I thought of last Christmas at Uncle William's house, with Mama and Daddy. We'd had a houseful of company. And gifts and a tree.

I was in another world now. A different time and place. I might as well be on another planet, I told myself. And then I wondered where I'd be next year.

BISHOP LAMY HAD WRITTEN the letter to my father, and Abeyta had been allowed to come and fetch it so that his father's courier could take it to Texas. Abeyta's appearance in the convent was much whispered about. He came early in the morning, and Elinora was allowed to see him in the Bishop's office, under his watchful eyes.

Some of the girls crept onto the stairway and came back upstairs, saying they'd actually seen him. It was almost as good as seeing Saint Joseph, for them. Or Jesse James. Afterward, of course, Elinora wouldn't speak of the encounter, though pressed by the other girls. She would say only that the Bishop had agreed to host a dance Christmas week, for the older boys and girls in the two schools.

Mail service in Santa Fe was always a haphazard business,

at best. The only thing that could really be counted on, people said, was the arrival of the army payroll, under escort from Fort Leavenworth, Kansas. There were government contracts to carry civilian mail between Santa Fe and the other territories and states. Before the war, mail came but twice a month. Now, at least, it came once a week—when the post wagon wasn't attacked by outriders.

That week before Christmas a letter came to me from Uncle William.

He was closing up his house in Independence for a while, to go to Kansas. "With my friend Jim Bridger," he wrote. "You are certainly welcome to come to Kansas when I become established, if you do not wish to live with your father. But I need at least six months to make a proper home for myself—let alone you—there."

Oh, Uncle William. I could see him already in Kansas with Bridger. I knew Bridger, bewhiskered and half blind by now. He'd had three Indian wives and six half-Indian children, all educated in missionary schools in Missouri. *What if I'd had my heart set on being with you, Uncle William? But the very thing I love about you—your independence—is what makes you not there for me now.*

Still, I knew he meant it when he said I could come in six months. He sent me books, writing paper, a silver frame with a photograph of my parents that had been taken in Independence, and an Indian blanket, for Christmas.

I was still waiting for a letter from Cassie. None came. (Later I was to find out that her letter was on a post wagon that had been attacked by Utes and Apaches in eastern New Mexico, and it ended up scattered with other mail across the Plains.)

All that week I hunkered down, like everybody else— studying, doing my chores, and missing Elena. We all missed her. A temporary home for her had been found with a good family outside Santa Fe. The Bishop was determined she should be safe and his school not endangered. He himself had visited Ramon Baca in jail, to tell him the child was elsewhere, without disclosing her whereabouts.

On Friday of that week, we had our first snow. It came quietly at the onset, then steadily, then quickly. An undercurrent of excitement ran through the school. And by the end of the day, the girls were running around squealing in delight. Within two hours there seemed to be three or four inches. I acted disinterested, even bored, as I considered it my duty to do. After all, I was from Missouri and we had our snows, didn't we? The day girls were dismissed early. By supper time there seemed to be seven or eight inches. It clung to everything, tree branches, walls, grillwork, lampposts. The robins flew into the cedar trees. The bluejays screeched and objected.

It was after supper hour. The choir was practicing in the dining room, where the tables had been pushed aside. There was about the place a general air of enclosed peace, yet an air of anticipation. As if something wonderful was about to happen.

It was the snow, I decided. These girls so seldom saw it, and from all Sister Roberta said, the sun would make quick work of it, and in a day or so it would be gone.

I was seated in the parlor next to the crackling fire, knitting a sweater for Elena. Cleo lay in a ball at my feet. I'd been to the barn and fed and seen to Ben. From down the hall came the muted strains of "Silent Night."

I looked up at the snow falling against the windows, and I felt a sense of peace such as I hadn't felt in months. More than peace, it was a flooding of contentment in my bones. As if I knew everything was going to turn out all right. For a moment I felt almost as if there was a presence in the room with me.

And then Cleo lifted her head, sniffed, stood up to arch her back, and hissed.

I am not a spiritual being. For all I had been through in Santa Fe, I still had no faith in uncommon powers of any kind. But at that moment I knew someone was in the room with me, some unseen presence, standing close, giving me assurances. Was it Mama? Mrs. Lacey? It was somebody. Or something. I was sure of it, and I didn't fight the sureness. I didn't scoff. And I didn't doubt. The knowing in itself was enough.

At that moment the door of the parlor burst open. Elinora stood there. "The staircase! It's finished!"

I jumped from my reverie and turned to look at her. "What?"

"It's finished! Ramona went just now to take the carpenter his supper. And found it completed. And he's gone."

I dropped my knitting from my lap and ran from the room.

THE OTHER GIRLS WERE already there. So were the nuns. They stood in the back of the church, gazing up at the staircase.

My mouth fell open. It was finished.

It rose in a graceful, swirling, polished circular arch, from the ground to the choir loft. The wood fair glowed in the candlelight, rich and burnished and solid. There were thirty-three steps. The girls were counting them. And each one was trimmed to perfection.

But it had no railing.

It had no supports. It seemed as if nothing was holding it up.

Sister Roberta was examining it. "Two complete three-hundred-and-sixty-degree swirls," she said. "It is spliced in seven places on the inside and nine on the outside. It is an incredible and impossible piece of work. No one man could have finished this in so short a space of time."

"But will it hold us?" Mother Magdalena asked in a near whisper.

"Well, there is one way to find out. And being the heaviest one here, I shall experiment," Sister Roberta said.

We all watched then, while she tentatively put one foot on the bottom step, smiled at us, then put a foot on the next step. Sister Catherine crossed herself. I saw Sister Hilaria mumbling silent prayers. Sister Roberta mounted the thirty-three steps, one by one, keeping her balance perfect for such a large body, and arrived at the top.

"Not one creak," she said as she stood up there above us at the entrance to the choir loft, "not one bit of swaying."

"Praise be," Mother Magdalena said. "We have ourselves a staircase."

"And from the looks of it," Sister Roberta said, leaning over to examine a step, "he didn't use nails, either. He used wooden pegs."

"Sister, don't fall," begged Mother Magdalena.

Sister Roberta straightened up. "Now, how do I get back down?"

I heard Mother Magdalena gasp, and the others murmur.

"Why didn't he make a banister?" Winona asked.

"Faith," said Sister Roberta. "He wanted to show us that we need faith. For now, I will come back down the only way I consider feasible. And afterward we will practice, so we can come down gracefully, showing our faith."

And with that she turned around and crept down, backward, step-by-step, on her hands and knees. There was even more praying now, then happy sighs when she reached the bottom. She stood up and turned to face us.

"The wood is beautiful," she said. "It is the most beautiful wood I have ever seen."

"It is so graceful," Mother Magdalena said, sighing. "It is like a prayer, lifting itself to heaven."

The nuns crossed themselves again. "What does this mean?" Sister Catherine asked.

"Yes, what does it mean?" asked Sister Hilaria.

Mother Magdalena turned to encompass us all with her gaze. "It can mean only one thing," she said. "Saint Joseph did come, after all. The carpenter man was Saint Joseph."

With that they all got down on their knees and started praying. I just stared at them all as if they'd taken leave of their senses. Then I ran from the chapel.

24

❀

OF COURSE, I DID NOT believe it was Saint Joseph.

The man had spoken to me. He had listened to my woes.
He had held my kitten and advised me about my father. He
had even told me how sad he was at having to leave his own
family. He had been hurt because the girls hadn't wanted him
around here.

Would a saint act like that?

Everyone had assumed that he had finished his work and
gone to the barn without supper because he was so tired. The
next morning I was up earlier than anybody, tracking through
the snow to the barn.

To feed Ben, I told myself. To walk him around the yard.
Later on I would beg Mother Magdalena to allow me to take
him for a ride on the road to the Bishop's farm, if not through
town. Even though I would have wanted to go to visit Mrs.
Lacey and Robert.

I fed Ben.

The carpenter was not in the barn. Neither was his mule. I asked Gregorio about him. He scratched his head and considered the matter for a moment.

"I came here to see the animals just after supper," he said, "to make sure they were all right. His mule was here then."

"And this morning?" I asked.

"It was gone. I am thinking he took his leave of us."

THE BISHOP CAME, summoned by the nuns. He examined the staircase, shook his head, pronounced it beautiful, looked properly puzzled, and told the excited girls he would have no hysteria, no fasting. "And I will accept no new callings," he said. He looked, significantly, at Elinora.

"And, please, don't let this get about just yet," he begged everyone. "Or we will have a tramping of people through here all day. Let us just keep our counsel. When people come to mass in the morning, they will see the staircase."

"And what will we say then?" Elinora asked.

"That we have a new staircase," he said.

"We should have a supper for the man," Mother Magdalena suggested, "to thank him properly. Is that all right with you, Bishop?"

"By all means."

"But he's gone," Winona wailed.

"He'll be back for his pay," the Bishop said.

"His mule is gone from the barn," I offered.

The Bishop looked at me. "You've come to know some of the merchants in town from your travels with Mrs. Lacey, haven't you, Lizzy?" he asked.

"Yes, Eminence."

"Then ask about today if anyone has seen him. Take some-one with you. Don't go alone."

"The lumberyard would be a good place to start," Sister Roberta suggested.

"Yes, start at the lumberyard. He was to use my account there," the Bishop said. "Sister Roberta will go with you, Lizzy. Take a horse, Sister."

And so it was that I saddled Ben, and Sister Roberta took a horse from the stables, and together we went about town that Saturday afternoon, to see if anyone had come in contact with the carpenter.

We first went to the lumberyard, where the man said no, the carpenter had never been there. He had never placed an order. The Bishop owed him no money.

"Then where did he get the wood?" Sister Roberta mur-mured.

The sun shown warm, already melting the snow. There was the excitement of the coming holiday in the air. We saw goods piled high, money exchanging hands; we smelled hot, fresh bread and coffee, roasting piñon nuts. Gaming tables were set up, and gentlemen of leisure and some soldiers were partaking in this vice. We asked at booth after booth. Some of the bazaar owners knew me because of Mrs. Lacey. Always, the answer was the same.

"No, we have not seen him."

"Nobody like that has been here."

On the way home we had to move our horses aside be-cause there was a horse race right on the street. I thought I rec-ognized one serape-draped young man as he dashed by on a magnificent steed. Yes, I was sure of it. It was Abeyta. Horse racing was illegal, but his father would pay the fine, if I knew anything about him from Elinora.

IT WAS DECIDED there would be a supper in the carpenter's honor, anyway. The following Wednesday evening. All the day girls would be asked to stay, and their parents would be invited.

There was to be stuffed turkey, wild duck, venison, fish, sweet potatoes, plum pudding, sweetmeats, syllabub. The Bishop was to preside. There was even rumor that he would wear his violet vest, something he did only at Christmas.

But the carpenter never came to collect his pay. The tubs he'd used to soak his wood in were nowhere on the property. Nor were his tools. And, of course, we never saw his mule again.

We had a fine dinner in his honor, anyway. And Bishop Lamy wore his violet vest.

FOUR MONTHS LATER, when I left the convent of Our Lady of Light, the tracks of the new Santa Fe Railroad came onto the plains of New Mexico, only sixty-five miles from Santa Fe. But I was not going that way. I was going to Texas.

Jesse James was in Nashville, Tennessee. There were no real outlaws in Texas anymore, but they did have the Texas Rangers. My daddy was an important manager on the Santa Gertrudis Ranch. He had his own adobe house with a nice courtyard. A Methodist circuit rider came through once a month. There was a school for the children on the ranch, and yes, I could bring Elena.

All my trip had been arranged by Bishop Lamy. Teresa Espinosa, Elena's wet nurse, and her husband, Georgio, and their baby boy were to accompany me. Along with an escort of six expert riflemen and scouts, supplied by Abeyta's father. There were three wagons in all.

It was a fine April morning. The apricot, cherry, peach, and pear trees were already in bloom. Lilacs were all around. Abeyta and Elinora stood, hand in hand, watching as I made ready to climb on Ben's back. Baby Elena was already sleeping in the back of the wagon.

Then, just before I mounted, Elinora grabbed my arm and whispered something into my ear. Had I heard her right?

I smiled down at everyone, from Ben's back.

I had my cat, my horse, my coin from Jesse James, my books and lessons from the sisters, food in great plenty from Ramona, and the blessing of Bishop Lamy himself, as well as his promise to come and visit.

There were waves and cheers. Then came the "gee" and "haw" and "wo ho," and we were off for the last time down the main street of Santa Fe. People stared at us and waved as we passed. And I was surprised to realize that I felt as if I were leaving home.

I WOULD MISS THEM, all of them. Even Elinora, whom I'd promised to invite to the ranch in the future.

But, had I heard her right?

There had been a lot of chatter and gay good-byes, but I know what she said. "I did prick your cat in the eyes that day. So if she's not blind—well, didn't you tell me that the carpenter held her?"

I sat, benumbed, on Ben, keeping pace with the wagons. For the last four months, everyone at the school and convent had persisted in believing that the carpenter had been Saint

Joseph. And I'd scoffed at the idea. After all, everything I was stood in the way of believing it.

People had come to see the staircase in droves. Local people and those from out of town. Experts in wood came to examine it and say they knew no wood like it within hundreds of miles around. The girls and the nuns would have their miracle, and they would hold on to it.

"How do you explain how quickly he built it?" they asked me. I said I didn't know. He was a good man. Maybe he sneaked helpers in the back door of the church at night. How did we know?

I knew only one thing. He wasn't Saint Joseph, that carpenter.

As for me, I'd witnessed miracles at Our Lady of Light, all right. Mrs. Lacey, for one. Bishop Lamy, for another. Sister Roberta. Maybe even, in the end, Elinora. And finally, the fact that my father wanted me.

I'd been happy with those miracles. They were enough for me. Until a few moments ago, when Elinora had whispered in my ear. She'd saved her best for last, to try to convince me, when I couldn't come back with a reply. Truth to tell, I didn't have one, anyway. I might never have one.

Now I saw Sister Roberta handing Cleo back to me that day, long months past, and saying, "She's blind." And I knew she'd been blind. And I saw José picking her up and looking at her in the barn and saying only, "She might see again. You must love her and care for her well."

Saint Joseph? Could he have been?

As we passed the hills that led to Fort Marcy, I looked up. Bishop Lamy had had the cemetery repaired. The day was warming. In the distance the Sangre de Cristo Mountains still had snow on top. But what drifted down on us now were the white seeds of the cottonwood drifts in the fields.

I heard Mrs. Lacey's laugh as we passed old Fort Marcy. "Those Polly Purehearts wouldn't know Saint Joseph if he did come."

Author's Note

❖

THE STAIRCASE IS A NOVEL based on one of the most famous legends in Santa Fe, that of the mysterious carpenter
who came to build a staircase in the Chapel of Loretto when,
with the completion of the chapel in 1878, it was discovered
that there was no way to get to the choir loft.

I have used the history of Santa Fe and this legend as a
springboard from which to write my fictional story.

The actual story goes that the Sisters of Loretto, brought
to Santa Fe in 1852 from Kentucky by Bishop Jean Baptiste
Lamy to run the Academy of Our Lady of Light, the girls
school attached to the chapel, consulted with many builders,
carpenters, and architects. They were told that a conventional
staircase to the choir loft would take up too much space and
that the choir loft should be rebuilt, at great expense, or a ladder used.

The sisters began a novena to Saint Joseph.

Then along came the beggar-man carpenter, with his mule
and only three tools, a hammer, a T square, and a saw. Some
accounts say he built the spiral staircase—which makes two

complete circles and has thirty-three steps—in two weeks. Others claim it was months. When it was finished, the nuns were so pleased, they planned a feast in his honor. But he was nowhere to be found. And men at the lumberyard where Bishop Lamy had an account for him said they had never seen him. He never came to collect his pay. He was never seen again.

The good sisters concluded that the carpenter beggar-man had been Saint Joseph.

To this day the staircase stands in the chapel, which Bishop Lamy had patterned after the Sainte-Chapelle in Paris. Gleaming and renowned, the only difference today is that it has a banister that was added in 1883.

It has been visited by people from all over the world. Made with wooden pegs and not nails, it has been examined over the years by many architectural experts, who cannot account for the wood used, and have determined that it is not to be found anywhere in New Mexico.

THAT IS THE BASIS of my novel. And, when my husband and I visited Santa Fe in 1999, this story of the staircase was immediately told to us by the shuttle driver as he took us from the airport to our hotel. To be sure, the Chapel of Loretto was one of the first stops in our tour of Santa Fe. I saw and touched the staircase. The story so intrigued me that one of my next stops was the local library, where I went through the clip files on the story and pursued the names of further books to read about the subject.

I knew immediately that I would do a book. The whole idea seemed to present itself to me "of a piece," as one would say in the eighteenth century. Especially when I heard of the girls school also run by the nuns under the direction of Bishop Lamy.

Of course, with the exception of Bishop Lamy, most of the characters I have used are of my own invention. Like Uncle William. But after extensive reading about Santa Fe at that time, including folklore and history, the characters seemed to literally take seed and grow in my mind.

From folklore I borrowed Lozen, woman warrior, and the witches who lived in town at the time. All represent the rich cultural traditions of nineteenth-century New Mexico. And Jesse James, a folk hero of the time to young girls, whose exploits were constantly in the newspapers and who was already himself a legend.

Santa Fe—indeed, all of New Mexico—can be summed up in the two words that seemed to appear in all studies: *spiritual* and *mysterious*. Indeed, mysteries abound that seem to grow out of the mix of Indian, Mexican, and Catholic beliefs and culture.

Imagine being a girl of thirteen seeing this place for the first time, after coming from the staid, workaday, small-town world of Independence, Missouri. Imagine having a father who lost one arm in the war, as well as his Georgia plantation. Imagine being displaced and abandoned here, the only Methodist in a houseful of Catholics, and having just lost your mother.

This is Lizzy Enders. Up until now her fantasy has been to meet Jesse James. Uprooted and placed in a convent in a neglected part of the American frontier, where boys wear dresses on the altar and she is surrounded by lifelike statues of bleeding saints, this Protestant girl from the Midwest finds she has stepped into a hornet's nest of intrigue, where miracles and visions are the order of the day.

I can clearly recollect being of such an age in Catholic school, when the graphic stories the nuns told us about the beheadings and torture of martyrs, and of Christians being devoured by lions, were a matter of everyday study. We were taught that to die for one's faith was the highest calling, that the most notable achievement in life was a happy death.

I remember wanting to have a vision even more than today's young girls want to see the latest pop star in person.

The next best thing, of course, was to have a calling. Just as clearly, I recollect the envy I and other girls felt when a girl announced she had one. And so, with such memories intact and with the wealth of research I did about Santa Fe, grew my story.

Having read Willa Cather's *Death Comes for the Archbishop*, which is about Bishop Jean Baptiste Lamy and his southwestern parish, I came away with nothing but admiration for the man, and I hope I have done him justice in my depiction. Mrs. Lacey is a combination of two people, one from research and one real. (The latter is a Catholic priest in Trenton, New Jersey's Spanish section, who could not walk down a street without being stopped by dozens of people. Once when I walked with him, he paused to either bless or give out money to half a dozen people.)

Elinora, of course, is every introspective young girl's childhood nemesis, the in-your-face rival who violates all rules, yet always seems to come out landing on her feet. The idea of having the girls conduct a hunger strike to get their own way in the school is mine. As is their initial rejection of the carpenter. But girls confined in a convent are not always devout, retiring, and repentant. More often they are rebellious, bored, and dying for adventure. And they will find it in the smallest distraction. They will make the most mundane cause an enchanted challenge.

For me this story had all the ingredients for intrigue. Yet, at the same time, it presented a challenge. Wandering in the unforgiving landscape of New Mexico at her tender age, Lizzy is bordering on becoming a lifetime cynic since her father ran off and her mother died. She nurtures a healthy disrespect of the bloody mysteries of Catholicism. She takes her miracles in small doses. To her, miracles are people: Bishop Lamy, Sister Roberta, even, at the end, Elinora. But most of all the very fact that her father eventually wants her.

Lizzy, whose girlhood soul is still only partially painted over with the graffiti of mistrust and doubt, must stand back from the general acceptance that the beggar-man carpenter she brought around was really Saint Joseph. Yet she must be left one small window of belief open to her—the blind cat, no longer blind since the carpenter held her. Does she believe when she leaves the convent? The jury is still out, as it is still out on the fact that the man who built the actual staircase was Saint Joseph. I wanted to leave it up to the reader to decide.

Lizzy Enders comes reluctantly to Santa Fe and the school, hoping only to find someday in her life her hero, Jesse James. She leaves a better person, yet not quite believing she has met Saint Joseph.

Bibliography

Cather, Willa. *Death Comes for the Archbishop*. New York: Vintage Books, 1990.

Hansen, Ron. *The Assassination of Jesse James by the Coward, Robert Ford*. New York: Alfred A. Knopf, 1983.

Hillerman, Tony, ed. *The Spell of New Mexico*. Albuquerque: University of New Mexico Press, 1976.

Kutz, Jack. *Mysteries and Miracles of New Mexico: Guide Book to the Genuinely Bizarre in the Land of Enchantment*. Corrales, N.M.: Rhombus Publishing Co., 1989.

Lamar, Howard R., ed. *The New Encyclopedia of the American West*. New Haven, Conn.: Yale University Press, 1998.

Magoffin, Susan Shelby. *Down the Santa Fe Trail and into Mexico*. New Haven, Conn.: Yale University Press, 1926.

Noble, David Grant, ed. *Santa Fe: History of an Ancient City*. Santa Fe: School of American Research Press, 1989.

Peters, Arthur King. *Seven Trails West*. New York: Abbeville Press, 1996.

Reiter, Joan Swallow. *The Women*. The Old West Series. Alexandria, Va.: Time-Life Books, 1978.

230

Russell, Marian. *Land of Enchantment; Memoirs of Marian Russell along the Santa Fé Trail.* Albuquerque: University of New Mexico Press, 1954.

Simmons, Mark. *Yesterday in Santa Fe: Episodes in a Turbulent History.* Western Legacy History Series. Santa Fe: Sunstone Press, 1989.

Tanner, Ogden. *The Ranchers.* The Old West Series. Alexandria, Va.: Time-Life Books, 1977.

Trachtman, Paul. *The Gunfighters,* The Old West Series. Alexandria, Va.: Time-Life Books, 1974.